G/11

STORM

New Writing from Mexico

STORM 7–8: New Writing from Mexico

Editor: Joanna Labon
Advising Editor in Mexico: Pedro Serrano
Assistant Editor: Alex Sapirstein

Cover painting by German Venegas, with thanks to the Galeria del Arte Moderna, Mexico City.

We gratefully acknowledge the assistance of the Arts Council of Great Britain and the British Council's Mexican office in this project.

Published by Storm

Printed by Expression, London

Distributed by Jonathan Cape Ltd,
20 Vauxhall Bridge Road, London SW1V 2SA

ISBN 0 224 03539 8

CONTENTS

Fabio Morábito, an Italian born in Alexandria, Egypt in 1955, settled in Mexico in 1969. He has published a volume of poetry, Lotes Baldíos, *a book of essays,* El viaje y la enfermedad, *as well as two works that defy easy classification:* Caja de herramientas*—part essay, part prose poem—and* Macrocefalia, *a collection of poems, short fiction, aphorisms and essays, written in collaboration with Adolfo Castañón and Jaime Moreno Villarreal. In these stories, taken from his most recent book,* Lenta Furia *(Slow Fury), Morábito imagines a summer of libidinous frenzy when a town's matriarchs sprawl naked on tree limbs awaiting their prey, and The Vetricciolis: a tribute to translators the world over.*

TWO STORIES FROM

SLOW FURY

by Fabio Morábito

THE VETRICCIOLIS

It is true that our numbers grew year upon year, but the old house on the Calle de Bolivar managed to accommodate us all comfortably, or rather in a comfort that grew subtler and more intimate by the day. Full of recesses and narrow corridors which suddenly and inexplicably broadened out, it seemed not so much a single house as an amalgam of many houses which had ended up jostling each other to occupy the same space.

Every corner boasted its desk, even if this was sometimes nothing more than a simple plank of wood on which to put a bookstand and an inkwell. Other desks were set up inside the family's huge old wardrobes, in window bays or on platforms built to take advantage of the high ceilings or any slight bulge in a corridor or room. Not a single cranny or gap in the walls was wasted. Desks were jammed into cramped recesses where there was scarcely enough room for a child and here, just as everywhere else in the house, work went on for ten or twelve hours a day by natural or artificial light. There were bedrooms upstairs, but at the end of the day it was common for many members of the Vetriccioli family to fall asleep, pen in hand, at their tiny desks.

Whenever a Vetriccioli came into the world, the older generation met in the basement to choose a workplace for the newborn: the west wing, the platforms in the south wing (where once there had been a kitchen), the levantine recesses or the central rotunda. And when a child reached the age of three he was put under the supervision of an uncle or an older cousin who introduced him to the bookstands, the drawers, the dizzy heights of platforms and dictionaries. By the age of six, every young Vetriccioli knew how to sit up straight, use a blotter, sharpen pencils, to rub out without chafing the paper, and tidy a desk. He was taught to take manuscripts from one platform to another, and to fill his cousins' and uncles' inkwells. At the end of each day he would proudly hold up his ink-stained fingers, and by the time he was seven he would be allowed to translate his first sentences and paragraphs which, as well as giving him practice, also helped determine which part of the family chain he would be best suited to fill.

For it was true that every translation we undertook passed from hand to hand until it had been revised countless times; each fresh pair of hands cancelled out the previous pair, and in turn were cancelled out by others. One platform annulled the work of another, one wardrobe another wardrobe, one wing of the house another wing. This caused delays in handing over manuscripts to the publishers, but by going through so many corrections and modifications, the work, like a good broth, acquired the taste and style of the whole family, that quality which experts could recognize at a glance and which made them exclaim admiringly, "That must be a Vetriccioli!"

It became considered good taste to mention our name together with that of the author, saying for example, "I've just bought a Molière-Vetriccioli", or "So-and-so gave me the latest Vetriccioli: Heine's *Florentine Nights*." People even said, "I've got a '42 Vetriccioli at home," without even bothering to mention what the book was or who had written it.

The Guarnieri family, who lived three blocks away in the Calle de Turin, tried to compete with us, and their speciality, which they advertised in the newspapers (they were so vulgar they placed advertisements in newspapers!) was for dead languages. But who can possibly decree the death of a language? Even though it may no longer be spoken or may only have flourished briefly, a language will never cease to resurface here and there, will always be part of the collective unconscious—that is why in our family it was often one of the youngest children, one who could barely lift a pen, who, perched up on some remote platform or other, worked out by pure instinct the origin of a word in an ancient Caucasian language or Turkistani dialect that had reduced his elders to despair. For us, nothing was obsolete, nothing had to be rescued from oblivion, because all language was made up of different layers continually shifting and settling, so that we thought the distinction the Guarnieris made between living and dead languages was nothing more than a ruse to push up their prices. What else was one to expect from a family that worked in a three-storey office block, people who did not live together, who undoubtedly competed with each other, who doubtless were not even all Guarnieris?

For our part, we never left the house. Even to cross a street one needs definite convictions, and as far as I know no Vetriccioli ever expressed anything remotely approaching a conviction or a general truth about anything not related to our work, or even criticized anyone else's conduct, apart from the Guarnieris' sharp practices. We were left cold by any ideas we came across in our manuscripts; we were concerned with the coherence of an argument only to enable us to translate it correctly, not to adopt or hoard it like the Guarnieris did. It was not hard to imagine the pedantic conversation in the Calle de Turin, full of arguments, unassailable principles, flaring passions, offended expressions! How different from our own conversations over dinner, full of witty repartee and digressions, where what was important was to hear ourselves all talk together and to perceive everyone's whims and secret inclinations, the chinking of their souls. We were always aware that we were nothing more than conveyor belts, and that is what enthused us. We lived in silhouette, half-responsible, half-alive. Our physique helped in this: both male and female Vetricciolis were always slender, not like the Guarnieris, who were as flabby as their prose. Not even the thinnest members of their family would have been at ease in the corridors and passageways of our house.

None of us had ever seen the whole house. Apart from its sheer size and its hundreds of twists and turns, the fervour of our work kept us from exploring. Anyone who undertook to reconnoitre it soon became bored; wherever he gave up he was assigned a desk either on a platform or on floor level where he could contribute most. Although infrequent, these migrations helped harmonize our style by putting in touch different sectors which over time had acquired their own characteristics. The levantine recesses were famous for the way they abused the passive voice and the semi-colon; anything which reached them that was at all lively and had a bouncy rhythm came out cautious and solemn. This became known as the levantine cadence, well suited to memoirs and the epistolary genre, but useless for happy or violent passages. A large part of the work of our great-great grandfather and the other elder generations who lived in the basement was to direct each transfer of the manuscripts to the most appropriate sector of the house. Nowhere better than the east wing for lyrical flights of fancy. Doubt, suspicion, and inner torment were the work of the southern platforms. The slightest variation in tone by the author (a nostalgic digression, a veiled suggestion of rancour) was enough to send the book speeding to the opposite end of the house, if only for a few lines. Each sector had its own strengths. One platform excelled in violent diatribes, another in the splutterings of rage. Every day the manuscripts passed through dozens of desks and were submitted to a morbid stylistic scrutiny. And just as no Vetriccioli had ever seen the whole house, so only a very few had read a manuscript from start to finish. I mean that for almost all of us, life was a question of short paragraphs, interrupted sentences. This prevented us from becoming emotional and losing control over the text, honing our sense of the value of every single word, but at the same time it made us less aware of its content and the development of the material. In the end, this led the eighth generation to completely lose any urge to converse over the dinner table. To them, the older generations' stories were a meaningless drone; they soon laid their heads on the long dining table and went to sleep. Whenever they spoke it was in fits and starts, completely devoid of emotion, and all at once they would fall silent as if they had never so much as opened their mouths. They were the tallest and thinnest of the family, maggot-white, like bits of string. They hardly even poked fun at the Guarnieris, or laughed. They barely consulted dictionaries or grammar books, and when they came up against a difficult passage, never asked for help but pulled in their feet and their stomachs, closed their eyes, took deep breaths and in a spirit of silent prayer found the word or syntactic expression to solve the problem.

When they toppled us, they did not unite, but amalgamated, because they did not trust each other either. Exasperated by the noise we made as we worked, their anger exploded one winter morning. They went down to our basement, where the first thing they did was to string up all the older generations. They took us all by surprise because our routine of desk work had slowed us up; many of us could not find the street door, others did not understand what was going on until they were hanging from a beam or platform, their feet scrabbling in the air; the few of us who succeeded in escaping did not join up again; each of us survived as best we could.

From that moment on, the Guarnieri family prospered as never before. They added a new floor to their office block in the Calle de Turin, and demanded they be credited in the books they translated. That vulgar custom has now become widespread. We would never have accepted seeing our name in print; the whole difficulty and dignity of our work consisted in convincing ourselves deep down that we did not really exist, in discovering that in fact the author knew Spanish, that secretly he had written in Spanish but due to some last minute accident had been forced to steep his work in another language, an outer layer which we unravelled like the bandages of an injured man. How each of the words gained in lightness and freshness as they were returned to their original mould! The Guarnieris fought to see their name in print and forgot that the secret of our task was a lengthy, caring rehabilitation process. We were there to heal wounds, to restore health and return things to their rightful place—nothing more.

Nowadays, when I creep along the garden wall in the Calle de Bolivar and pause for a couple of minutes outside the empty, tumble-down old house (as was to be expected, blind and deaf as they were, they soon destroyed each other just as they had destroyed us, but I always made sure I picked up the post from the letter-box at the front of the house and dispatched it as carefully as possible in order to foil any suspicions or awkward questions), I can see them all again: Great-grandfather Julio, Aunt Sampdoria and Uncle Cornelio; my brothers Pilade and

STORM 7–8/ 1992

Edgardo, all my cousins and uncles from the central rotunda, cursing, cackling, screwing up their eyes in their effort to find the perfect adjective or the most elegant turn of phrase. Every sector was caught up in the same passion for perfection, and even though our numbers grew with each year, the house, with a corner here, an indentation there, always offered a hidden fold or undiscovered corner for a new Vetriccioli. Of course one had to get used to the fresh arrivals, to make room for them, to become imperceptibly thinner, to keep one's arms tucked in as one wrote, to consult dictionaries as little as possible to avoid disturbing others, to be more precise, more exacting in the choice of words: in short, to move around only when strictly necessary. So each new Vetriccioli brought with him a subtle readjustment, an almost invisible change in tone and style, in the same way that old members of the family when they died took with them words and cadences that were lost forever. What we all shared was a passion for our work, our devotion to the house and the realization that we were inventing nothing at all, simply working on what had already been elaborated by others, correcting only to be corrected in turn by others, aware that originality did not exist and that no personal touch had any value, which meant it had to be eradicated, and that this was the essential difference between us and the Guarnieris, between their flabbiness and our agility, between their office block and our old house in Bolivar, where one ended up getting lost in its thousands of twists and turns.

translated by Nick Caistor

Fabio Morábito

THE MOTHERS

It would begin in the first days of June, sometimes earlier, sometimes later. Whatever the exact date, it was really unpleasant to find yourself playing in a friend's house and suddenly, just when he had gone to the toilet or to the kitchen for a glass of water, his mother would emerge from the bedroom next door, stark naked and hot for it. You had to take her on with no help at all, because she would almost always shut herself up in the room with you and bolt the door. We'd been taught to thump the mothers on the chest, the head, or the belly, but some of them were really strong; others were as supple as deer, others still so fat that all they had to do was squash us until we gave in and did whatever they desired.

To be in a mother's power meant staying in her clutches for the whole of the month of June. After sundown you had to be on the lookout for the ones who were perched up in the trees. They usually lay naked, their breasts gorged, along one of the branches, while the kids had a fine time shooting at them with their catapults. If any of the mothers looked as though she was about to climb down from her tree, everyone withdrew to the pavement opposite to watch her descend, covered in cuts and bruises from constant rubbing against the tree bark.

The mothers spent most of their time up in the trees that lined the city streets, moaning with desire, shaking the branches.

At dusk, most of them climbed down and

curled up for the night in doorways. Their children used this respite to tend their wounds, take them food, cover them with blankets. Many mothers woke up later in the night and began to wander around aimlessly, or rather with the only aim that kept them alive: to be possessed, shaken to the core, clawed at. They became more and more truculent and cunning, running stealthily, setting ambushes.

With the first light of day, the panting of mothers as they overpowered their prey could be heard from pieces of waste ground and building sites all over the city. You could approach without fear because a mother who already had her victim was not dangerous. Caught in the pincer of her massive thighs, he wriggled like a worm in a bird's beak. The mother could have her way with him for the whole of June.

Mothers who had still not caught their prey lay in wait in the trees, wet and dripping. They had slippery, flabby bellies; whenever one of them fell out of a tree all you could hear was a faint "plop", then you'd see them swing back up into the branches without so much as a scratch on them. Sometimes they let themselves fall on purpose, to calm their fever, and they'd lie there soft and steaming, like flotsam left by the retreating tide. This state of complete abandon inflamed the men, who trembled at the mere sight of them. To mate with a mother in this state was to plumb the depths of vulgar depravity. The mothers could tell at a glance all those who had fallen into this trap in previous years. They knew how to deal with them! They ordered them to crawl to their feet; pitifully, the men obeyed, in full view of everyone, powerless to control themselves. A jab with the heel to the back of the head or shoulders was the only reward these unfortunates received.

The mothers also clambered up the railings, balconies, the beams of unfinished buildings. Council workers put out big cauldrons of water and food for them. The mothers swarmed down, starving, pushing and scratching at each other to get the best positions. At once all the kids in the windows of the nearby flats got out their catapults and bombarded them with pebbles or tiny pieces of glass, wounding them pitilessly despite their howls of rage.

At the end of June, the mothers slowly began to calm down, to dry out. Gradually, one after another, they allowed themselves to be dragged back to their homes. The whole city took on an air of religious reclusion. Indoors, children and husbands washed them lovingly, cleansed their wounds and watched over them as they slept (a sleep which sometimes lasted for as long as four or five days). Everyone walked respectfully on tiptoe so as not to wake them; all the rooms were kept dark to protect their sleep: even the family pets were on their best behaviour. Work in offices and factories was at a strict minimum in order to ensure the mothers got the best possible care. Hardly anyone went out except to buy provisions or medicine.

When the mothers woke up, recovered from their wounds, the penetrating stench of their frenzy had cleared from the city. You could see them at household chores on their balconies, some in housecoats, others dressed to go out and do the shopping. There they were, shaking out the sheets, watering the plants or shouting advice to their children as they scurried off to school. Factory chimneys belched out smoke at full tilt once more, trams screeched around the curves, people argued and fought at the slightest excuse. In the streets, even stray dogs went about their business with renewed gusto. The usual hubbub filled the morning air; nobody seemed to remember the chaos and anguish of the days gone by. Nobody said a word about it. But in the trees where the mothers had lain in wait, wet and frenzied, there now hung the huge ripe fruits of summer.

translated by Nick Caistor

STORM 1:

"An impressive début... real treasures to prise out from between the covers."
Literary Review

THE PEOPLE NEXT DOOR
by Sophie Basch
OUR AFTERNOON WALK
by Péter Nádas
THE GOLDEN BOY
by Helga Schubert
MESHUGA STUNDE
by Bohumil Hrabal
SWALLOWING GEOGRAPHY
by Deborah Levy
THE PERMANENT GUESTS
by Nick Drake
THE SUB-TENANT
by Hanna Krall
THE PLOUGHMAN'S LUCK
by Adam Bodor

Jaime Moreno Villarreal was born in Mexico in 1956. An author and an academic, he has published a number of books, including La Estrella imbécil, *a volume of poetry, and* La Habitacion interminable, *a collection of essays written in collaboration with Xavier Guzman Urbiola. In this story, a young girl makes a rite of passage which is usually left to the boys as, through a child's eyes we see childhood carted away.*

FIRST BLOOD
by Jaime Moreno Villarreal

Once we'd come around the bend at La Airosa, we spotted the customs shed straight ahead at the side of the road. You had to stop. The flat landscape decreased after the shed and everything looked intimidating. A customs officer always peered in through the window and we'd usually be carrying something prohibited, either smoked turkey or an electric lamp, an errand for some relative at Dos Ejidos, which made us accomplices. My grandmother slowed down and called out to me through the driving mirror, stretch out flat so they don't see the arms, there's a good girl. I rode atop two rifles covered by an oilskin coat. Next to my grandmother was my uncle Rene, who had the beard of an unlucky man. My grandmother drew up alongside the shed as she was obliged to. It was one of those houses you pass on a journey, which you think you'd like to live in. It had a well, a poultry run, high walls, a wash-house and a latrine. But there wasn't a soul about. Who's going to check us, my grandmother asked, opening the car door and alighting, while Rene was saying, let's get a move on, Mother. My grandmother went to look inside the house. She called, disappeared within and came out saying, well, there were people here quite recently, but there's nobody here now. She started up and we continued on our way. How are you? She was looking at me in the mirror, nothing new, I with an arsenal under my back and backside. There was quite a smell in there, she said, policemen always smell of sweaty feet. What they smell of is rank ill-gotten money, Rene cut in, tucking his pants inside those boots of his which he never took off. I knelt on the seat and watched the small house receding, thinking, dirty old men. Everything became tiny. What I mean, Mother, is they'll take your guns away from you and then go off and sell them. Who knows what they'll get up to—and then hold you responsible. I felt myself shrinking away from the rifles. That's what killing in cold blood will be like, I thought; coming in contact with the carbine's metal had made me shiver. Before worrying about the quarry you have to check your weapon, Rene was saying. The cigarette he was smoking slightly disguised the trace of beer on his breath. A good hunter never leaves his gun. Rene boasted of having killed bears and deer when he was young. Bears and deer are thin on the ground now, stated my grandmother, and I never saw a rug or a real pair of horns in my house. My uncle agreed, laughing. I'd already learned that anything Rene had done in his life, he'd done as a lad. He was always dressed in working clothes—a shirt with little-devil studs and cowboy trousers—but in fact he did nothing except drive his car around the streets of Bagdad. He cruised up and down in his little blue Renault all day with no set purpose, came back to eat, then went away again. And when my grandmother and I went out to buy rice or to get some air, we'd see his little car negotiating the potholes. At the time, over the border, there was a new car called the Toronado. My grandmother gave this little blue one the nick-name of Tronado*, and so as not to arouse suspicion in the customs shed she always took over the steering wheel. That afternoon, without stopping to visit our relatives, we passed the turning for Dos Ejidos, then the water tower and the River Purificación. This is all right, come on, turn here, Mother. We left the main highway and then Rene took over the wheel and started to take short cuts. It was fun going with Rene because it was always a little scary. I glued myself to the back window when my grandmother said, if you don't keep your eyes open you'll go home with an empty basket, let's see if something shows up in the fields. Sure enough, there'd soon be the brown and yellow streak of some animal's fur, but for the moment only the engine noise and the dust filled my soul, and finally we came to the boundary of an estate, the Capomo ranch. Get out, Finita. I opened the heavy gate, the car went through and I shut it again. In the distance, tractors were ploughing and a flock of herons was prospering in the wake of the machines. They'd be good for a partridge shoot, said Rene. We cut across by the ranch house. Some shy little children peeped out, they were playing with tools like adults, and our small blue car gave the dogs and roosters a fright. We drew away from where the people were and the car picked up speed as if to say it preferred potholes and dips in the road. Right, Finita, we're going to show you how to load that rifle. We were in uninhabited country. We got out. He put a rifle in my hands, opened the chamber, filled it with shot and showed me the safety catch, like so, as good as God, like so, devil's work afoot, and when you're carrying it, never keep your finger on the trigger because you'll blow your foot off or slaughter a cloud or you'll have bad luck. We went back to the car. I stuck the barrel out of the window, and we started up with a jerk and he stepped on the gas until we came to another gate, belonging to the El Caballerato ranch, all run down and irregularly planted. From our trail other paths fanned out, cutting strips into arable land, paths suggested at the edge of ravines and the old tracks of station-wagons at the side of irrigation channels, trails that forded, crossed and took short cuts choosing ways that let us penetrate deeper into scrubland and muddy places, travelling through a very sparsely cultivated world.

There it is. What? He stopped the car, turned off the engine. I didn't notice at first. Hand over the carbine, Finita, but carefully. The shadow didn't reveal details, a blaze of green and black, and I thought I distinctly saw a wild beast with tusks in the distance. Rene told me it was time to get out. Where, Uncle? There in front. I don't see anything. Finita, what can you see? my grandmother muttered as she got out. The eagle in the tree. Very black, brilliant, an eagle which overlooked the world and sifted the light, an eagle perched on a branch on top of the body of an animal bigger than a hare, remains which looked like a goat's. Take good care of this girl for me. My uncle made me rest the rifle on top of the car's bonnet, aim at the breast. I lodged the weapon firmly against my shoulder, supported the barrel, my uncle released the safety catch, and I looked through the sights. I fired. Ten yards away like a harpy it opened out and flapped for all its worth, but it didn't fly away, there it was, looming bigger and blacker. I pressed the trigger again. A menacing spread, and it was having a high old time with its beak, but it neither fell nor soared. It can't move, Rene said, it's full of food. Get a little closer. Supporting myself now on my legs, at last I felt more like a hunter, firm on my feet, my legs a squad, my chest an arch. I fired again, urged on by my uncle, one shot more and it more than fell. We didn't recover the specimen, dead with its prey, stinking. Another smell of blood. All right, now I've killed, and that was the deal.

It was my birthday. My grandmother used to let me climb trees, ride bareback, swim in the river, that sort of thing, but going out shooting, no, only the men. That month I had my first period, and I saw a cloud of prohibitions approaching, so that my birthday present was to do what I still had to do, namely to kill. My grandmother said no, why do you want to act like a man, but when Rene suggested that the two of us could accompany her to look for deer, she became excited. After all, she'd never been out hunting either. As a child she had run through a hail of bullets and seen disarmed men executed, but she'd never held a firearm in her hand. If they ask you, Finita, tell them it's just a sudden whim of mine. To shoot deer. But that afternoon, after killing the eagle, I was no longer in the mood. Rene went up to the disgusting eagle and, pulling a face, he came back to the car like a man-eating tiger, eager to shoot at whatever he came across. Again, he forced us round the trails he knew. We silently disembarked at last in a flooded expanse which was neither a reservoir nor a marsh, one of those large pieces of land which became impossible to cultivate after the rains. My uncle picked up his shotgun from the seat and loaded it. He told us there were duck among the reeds and that we should both keep very quiet. It could be important for me, but he was urging my grandmother to let fly with her gunpowder. Rene lowered his voice and gave her directions. Look, take the rifle. Just keep looking over there. Don't make a noise. My grandmother was like a genuine bandit, watching for aircraft in the sky. Where do I aim, what at? she whispered urgently. My uncle, raising his own gun in turn, told her, when I say fire, Mother, just shoot over there. What do you mean over there, don't confuse me. My uncle was getting ready. Now, just shoot in the air, come on. Well, my grandmother shot into the air, letting out a yell. Sure enough, some ducks rose in flight and Rene shot at them repeatedly while they were on the wing. Seeing two or three of them fall didn't upset me at first, but with bated breath I followed the ones which, though wounded, went flapping away beyond the tumult and seemed to be going off to fall to earth out of reach, or those which, caught by the shot, carried on without falling, sometimes they even rose. The recoil had slightly hurt my grandmother's shoulder and she said grumpily, I don't like duck, even quail's hardly worth eating, so on this occasion too my uncle didn't recover any game. But I took a small, grey, wounded duck back to the car. It was shedding feathers because of its wound and I held it between my legs, staining myself with blood, and stroking it as if I could cure it until some thin little membranes dried over its open eyes and it was dead, still warm in my hands. I would have liked it as my own little pet, to cure it and to give it back to the water. I want you to take me to kill a deer, my grandmother demanded, her bad shoulder pestering her as we started off. What are you thinking of, Mother, kill a deer? Where would we put it in this car? Well, just don't make me shoot into the air like an idiot, stupid.

I kept the duck in my lap while we climbed the rise and went across the plain. What are you doing with that animal? my grandmother asked. Get rid of it at once, I don't know how to cook it. If you don't, I'm going to throw it on the rubbish dump as soon as we get home. A row of very tall palm trees rose up in the distance, shore creatures. They formed a border with the sierra, there was neither level ground nor agricultural land beyond. It was as if the sea was on the other side. My grandmother said she could taste salt in the air. The way through the mountains eluded us. The afternoon was fading. Rene was telling hunting stories. He recounted a deer hunt with his buddy Abel, the night when they strayed from the camp where they'd put up their tent and built a fire. They went on foot, lighting their way with a battery lamp, no road, no moon, no deer. And to make matters worse, mist. Then the batteries ran out. My uncle tripped in some thickets and lost his nice wristwatch. Abel helped him up and they went on walking one behind the other, touching and listening out for one another until one of them went the wrong way. Abel, where are you? asked Rene. I think we'd better stop here. But his friend didn't answer. Where are you, Abel? Nothing, only a bird screeching. Well, Rene went on wandering alone, until desperation in the blackness overcame him by some brambles. There he fell asleep. But something soon wakes him—a slight noise by his ear. Tick-tock. He stretches out his hand and finds his watch hanging on a bramble. He reaches out to recover it and at that moment the earth begins to tremble. The earth rises up and he tries to hold on, grabbing at the surrounding branches. Everything is shaking and shifting, the earth's moving. Then Rene realizes that in fact he's riding on the back of a deer, and he starts to manoeuvre the animal as best he can, by its horns, where his watch is hanging, and so he returns, riding triumphant into camp. Rene was turning the Renault's steering wheel this way and that, as if jockeying his deer towards the camp fire, and the sun was turning yellow.

We turned down a road towards an irrigation canal, not very full at the time. The duck began to grow cold in my hands and I wanted to get home. We drove along the edge of the canal. I was looking at the necks of my uncle and my grandmother, and it came to me that one day the skin of my hands would be burnt and wrinkled in the same way. We were going to get through the evening without killing any deer. The three of us had let no more than a minute go by without speaking and it was already growing dark. Suddenly a multi-storey white building stood out against the setting sun at the end of the canal. The surrounding land looked parched. The building evoked a municipal clock in the desert. It's a Protestant church, my grandmother said. Rene laughed very softly. The things you think of, Mother, and he drove the small blue car onto the apron which enclosed the headwaters of the canal. This is called La Aljama, Rene explained, and that building was a meteorological station, it's been abandoned since they built Bagdad airport. Well, I can't believe there'll be deer hereabouts, my grandmother decided. Well, no, forget about deer, we're after heron, the quarry my uncle preferred, white heron with beaks sharp as darts. How do you know there are any? I can't see a thing.

Behind the towering building with its big broken windows, twilight was closing in. The small dam was sunk into a rocky bed. On the lookout for the likely mantle of herons, we approached on foot along the bank which sloped down to still water. The light's reflections gave the impression of solid masses lying on top of the reservoir's waves. I carried the carbine on my shoulder. Rene went ahead carrying the shotgun, looking for the best place to climb down. When we were almost level with the water, my grandmother and I stopped. She was very tired and didn't want to go any further, nor were there any herons in sight, so I followed my uncle alone. We skirted around stones. A cold breeze was blowing and I thought about the hunt in the dark with his friend Abel. Noticing something floating near the other bank, Rene halted suddenly. We could make out the shapes of some large animals, like seals, which seemed to be bathing on that side. Like fallen round rocks.

They were two darkish animals, like half-submerged walruses, with gleaming wet backs. Keep quiet, Finita, he said excitedly. We approached. Our weapons weren't meant for this type of game, I thought, what, then, was my uncle after? They're very big for badgers, Rene said, but they are not lions. You must shoot them from a long way off because they could be dangerous, I was thinking, or rather shoot them close up so as to get them in the heart or the head, or better still leave them in peace. Twenty yards away, with the light dying, we positioned ourselves like riflemen to mow them down from our bank. Bullets and shot which didn't hit their bulk splashed into the water. The animals' bodies stirred under the impact. They're bears, Rene guessed. But they didn't attack us, though I'm sure they went on bleeding until there was no more light.

My grandmother was already waiting in the car. What did you kill, child? Rene finished his shoot without recovering a single piece. To cap it all my grandmother revealed that when we started shooting, some herons rose up in flight on this side, a good hundred of them. Rene was in a bad mood, who knows what he'd killed. What with short cuts, we were eating up the road, and when it was completely dark, we saw rivetted on the windscreen the two shining eyes of an animal caught in the headlights. It's a hare, or a pheasant, my grandmother insisted. Two big eyes surprised by the Renault's bigger eyes. It's a deer, I said, I was absolutely sure. As the headlights advanced, illuminating it, it turned out to be a ranch dog. If it'd been a coyote, it'd be dead already, Rene shouted, assailing it with the horn. I still had the carbine's barrel stuck out of the window. My finger was on the trigger. I wondered whether or not the safety catch was on. I pressed, and the report resounded in our bones. Josefina! This shooting party's over once and for all, my grandmother growled. And Rene addressed me very seriously. If I'd done that when I was out hunting with your grandfather, he would've boxed my ears.

We reached the highway for the journey home. Before we mounted the asphalt, my grandmother helped me to conceal the guns on the seat, and again she took the wheel. Rene lit a cigarette, presenting a firefly to the night. I began to feel sleepy.

I woke up when my grandmother braked near Bagdad. At the end of a line of vans and buses they were checking. Reinforcements. Rene told me to lie down properly on top of the guns, and he covered me with the oilskin. Pretend to be asleep, Finita. I shut my eyes. I felt the cold of the barrels again, callous. When the troop reached us, I heard a policeman lean in through the window. Where have you come from? Dos Ejidos, my grandmother replied. What are you carrying? Nothing, sir, she and Rene said at one and the same time. We'll see. Open the boot. My uncle got out and I heard them talking together. He shut the boot and got back into the car. Rene told my grandmother under his breath that the two guards at the customs shed had, it seemed, disappeared, they were not to be found, they must have been killed. I saw an officer lean through Rene's window. What have you got there? It's my granddaughter, sir. My grandmother uncovered my chest. What is that child carrying? The officer shone his torch on me. I stiffened against the weapons, pretending to be waking up. I had the dead duck in my hands. It's a poor little bird, said my grandmother. We're going to bury it.

translated by Anthony Edkins

★ An untranslateable pun: Toronado is a car of American make; *tronado* means broken down or useless—AE.

STORM 2:

"An attractive new publishing venture."
London Review of Books

BERLIN DIARY
by Desmond Hogan
THE LAND AT THE NEXT TABLE
by Herta Müller
MRS KADLECKOVA
by Eda Kriseová
THE BOOK OF NUMBERS
by Pawel Huelle
TWO POEMS
by Tamara Szaniawska
BREAD, 1956
by László Petrovics-Ofner
AUNT FRANCES
by Péter Kántor
THE GOSPEL OF VALESKA
by Irmtraud Morgner

Regina Cohen was born in New York in 1955 and has been living in Mexico since the age of six. A graduate in Social Anthropology, she received the Fiction Award from the Fine Arts National Institute in 1982. She has published four collections of fiction, including Los Tígres Están Ahí *(1983)* , Adentro Al Fuego *(1985) and stories for children. In Almost Pure, she juxtaposes past and present, male and female, internal and external voices often in one sentence, to evoke rhythms of seduction and loss which are tinged with Catholic guilt and the restrictions of "machismo".*

Almost Pure

by Regina Cohen

I always followed you with my eyes, smiling roguishly; she's looking fabulous, he remarked to his friends, adding: and besides, I like her. Then she arrived, sat down crossing her legs, adjusted her skirt with her hands, pulled it down to cover her knees, asked for a coffee, felt conspicuous.

He stopped her on the way out of the café, offered to take her home. No, thank you very much, I like walking, then I'll come with you, he insisted. How've you been, he asked, she replied that she was well, that's obvious, he retorted. They arrived at her house, she said goodbye without shaking hands, slowly went up the steps, holding her skirt so the wind wouldn't expose her, and in she went.

I persuaded her to go for a drive, let's go to Chapultepec, she presumed he meant to his friends, to see how I'd get on. He called for her at seven, they got into the car, he did most of the talking, I've been watching you, I think you're shy, but it's a special kind of shyness, you know, there's a certain sauciness about it, and she smiled. They carried on talking, until he started to feel cold, aren't you cold? No, she said sharply; they arrived at the park, walked round the lake, he promised her the earth, then tried to take her in his arms. No thank you, I'm fine as I am, but you could tell a mile away she was cold, so after the walk we got back into the car but I didn't start the engine, I edged closer and closer, and without giving her a chance to refuse slipped my arm round her shoulders, she shook her head and folded her arms defensively. You've got beautiful legs, he remarked, she nodded, pressing her knees firmly together, and adjusting her skirt to cover them. I didn't even manage to give her a kiss, she kept avoiding my eyes, she wouldn't let me kiss her either then or on the sixth successive date.

On the seventh (Chapultepec again), I didn't get out of the car, I didn't even ask her to come for a walk, I looked at her breasts beneath her blouse as I was talking, and she sat quite still, eyes down, all she offered were isolated words, and an occasional smile; you're looking very pretty, (and getting closer), I'm crazy about you, (quite softly), let me see you, look at me darling, then he gently turns her head as their lips almost met. She trembles slightly and draws back towards the door, then turns abruptly and looks out of the window. Is something the matter with you? he asked. Nothing, and she wouldn't say any more. Upset, she tried to leave him, but he stopped her getting out of the car, I'm sorry if I upset you, I didn't mean to, and she silent, I don't want to offend you, but I just had to kiss you, look, the truth is, I couldn't help myself, and finally, the thing is I love you, you do understand that, don't you? Her expression mellowed, she smiled and said goodnight.

They met once a week, always the park, the same fountains, night reminding him of her fully-clothed body with every step and turn, of her timid way of sitting all hunched with her arms folded, and her legs, sit properly, child straighten your skirt and would you please do up your blouse, it's getting cold. I'm not cold, she repeated sharply, I'm fine as I am, and she folded her arms again, he embraced her all the same, and she relented just a bit, moving away from him as she felt his fingers slip towards her breasts: still this tepidness, she's scared of pleasure. They can see us, she said accusingly. There's no one about at this hour, I've been here before, he told her, reaching out and touching her gently, no one can see us, he slowly caressed her, alluring her with unknown possibilities, while she is impassive, expectant, unable to surrender, unable to rebuff him, only just for a moment, just for an instant, her legs quivered; she pulled away his hand which played under her blouse, gave him a furious look, and was silent. You're frightened of me, I'm not going to hurt you, why shouldn't I caress you, there's nothing wrong in that, I've already given you a kiss and nothing happened, now did it? She seemed frozen except at those moments when he coaxed a muffled sigh from her, a faint trembling, followed by passive retreat, into her shell again, legs together, skirt in place, I've told you already, do up your blouse, it's getting cold and your bra's showing; legs pressed together, when he probed under her skirt, slowly her thighs, on a cold night, alone, nobody can see us, relax, conversing with her legs, they're beautiful, they're like honey; she letting herself go a little, just my legs, she said. Yes, he reassured her, just your legs, but imagining it was all of her, getting to know her again bit by bit, in desperation.

The desire to hold her close became more and more oppressive, to explore her slowly, to unlock her sensuality, to conquer her hesitation, let yourself go, enjoy yourself my sweet, he wanted to capture even her fragrance, and begged sometimes gently sometimes firmly: I want to love you, to be alone with you, in the car I can't have you the way I'd like, nor do I feel you're completely at ease, you're always so defensive, but she replied that she wouldn't, that she wasn't that sort of girl.

Where are you going, she inquired apprehensively, this is the road to Toluca, not to Chapultepec. A surprise, he said and accelerated. He stopped at a motel on the side of the road and drove into the car park. Let's leave this place, she begged, I'm not getting out of the car. It's as if you don't love me, he reproached her, I've never done you any harm, my dear, I want to be alone with you, where no one can see us, you'd feel calmer, but she wouldn't have any of it, not before we're married, and I'm going to wear white, I've already told you. All right, all right, I know, and tempering his voice: we'll do the same as we always do, that's all, I promise you.

He got out, paid for the room and went back for her, giving her a little tap on the cheek to encourage her. Her coat seemed to cover her completely, as she sank her head down between her shoulders, guilty, but not wanting to annoy him, or to lose him.

They went up the stairs, he quickly, she trembling: she could feel threatening eyes staring at her from behind the bolted doors, from the tenuous light of the corridor which led to the end room, overwhelmed by a feeling of helplessness.

Don't be afraid, come, sit down beside me, take off your coat, but she wouldn't, she was cold, and he flatly, I'll take it off, come and give me a hug, stop worrying, no one can see us, but the eyes were watching her through the curtains, through the mirror, frightening her. He took off her coat, her blouse, tries to unfasten her bra, she covers herself with her arms, moves away, stops him stroking her, night after night; his audacious hands exploring her extremities, her nooks her crannies, the hours pass by. Your tears begging me: enough, you do love him, but not as far as that, you swore, you promised you'd look after me, as he kissed her very gently, moistening her face which she dried with her hand, searching for her legs between the sheets, and now he takes off her stockings, another day he fondles her hair, her subjugated breasts, her stomach, throws her clothes to the foot of the bed, stripping away her modesty, drop by drop until he's got her before him completely naked several months later, always promising that he'll never hurt her, only touch her, smell her, look at her, look at you, get to know you better, my darling, just as I got to know your naked lips, your neck, in the beginning, and nothing happened, don't be afraid, I won't hurt you; all huddled up, listening, covering your nakedness with the sheets to shield you from the eyes piercing through the window, your hands like playful little fish hover round you, then he naked as well, lying beside you, the two of us together from the waist upwards, this close no more, because she won't allow it, she won't let him, or the story would be different, but it's like this because she's afraid of losing him, thus conditionally, because he promised, you swore you'd respect me, but open your legs, let me see you, just for a moment, now shut them again, like a well brought up little girl, guilty, accepting the burning warmth of his masculine body, just because you're cold, and you don't want to be left alone, not again.

He asks if he can look at her, let me admire you, turn round, he takes her in his arms, throws her on the bed and plays with her, talks about the present, about love, about her body. He gradually strips her, snatching from her the closeness she lavishes at times, always guilty, feeling dirty, specially after consenting to stroke his masculinity, to let me feel you with it between your legs; little fish surround your dwelling place, pass by near you, occasionally sniffing you, making your pores open, making you move like a siren through the waters, impenetrable, but dirty, sensitive to the burning caresses, to the legs which envelope you, to the kisses which scorch your skin without managing to obliterate the beginning of your sin, which started when you felt you were lost, threatened by his absence, by his desertion, by the lack of gentle words which diminish your existence.

She looked at him without understanding when he set her a time limit, her last chance to respond or he'd leave her; she wept innocently, distant, fear enveloped her, hugging her, licking her, the little damp fish hovered around her, smelling the place between her legs from time to time, only to go away alone, insulting you, siren, cursing you, unconquerable, hungrily demanding your body, that you should feel it fully as he wanted and start a different story, but she kept on saying no, when we're married, she kept repeating despite her fear of losing him, but even more for fear of being weak, of letting herself be led on by his soft words which she so much needed, of taking a false step and plunging to the depths, of consenting and being rejected by him for ever, that's what loose women deserve, don't ever let a man put his arms around you again, it may tempt desire, did you understand or shall I repeat it so it's quite clear? Understand that love can't be like this, he kept saying, as he probed you, trying to break you, siren, to satisfy his obsession, consuming you in unfinished sin, savouring your smell, your hairs, you falling like any common woman, you thought, but he gently, enveloped you, hoping to be able to crouch on top of you, to scrape off your scales, siren, you began to hate him enough to bite him, your valley began to sprout teeth which stopped him from inhabiting you, resisting the last stage of your downfall, but without being able to put the breaks on or abandon him, because he kept saying he loved you, that's why he was giving you that one last chance, and you imagined yourself a sacrificial lamb already bleeding, already dead.

Tomorrow, he cautioned her, tomorrow—but the following day she refused again because she was already worthless in his eyes, you'd no longer want me, you'd reject me, and the eyes looking at her through the window, punishing her, watching him leave, leaving her in number forty-seven, while she shouts like a woman gone mad, a siren without a soul, the fish fled, the eyes watch furtively from behind bolted doors watching you sink, drop by drop in your own tears. If you'd only agreed, everything would have been different, you'd have both been truly happy, yet you a whore, you thought, the eyes from the mirror as sole witness of your desolation that night, knowing also that it would have been different, that you wouldn't have woken up tossed to the foot of the bed, with a saintly grin on your face, my siren, for having saved yourself from falling to the depths, but with your fingers poking your walls, and your legs wide apart, yes now.

translated by David Graham-Young

STORM 3:

"STORM is a bold young quarterly which offers a berth to challenging writing from East and West."
The Times

COUNTESS HAHN HAHN
by Péter Esterházy
SCHOOLBOOKS
by Dubravka Ugresic
ON THE BATTLEFRONT
by Alaine Polcz
THE WHIRLPOOLS AND LUCYNELLA
by Urszula Benka
AUNT FRUZIA
by Jerzy Ficowski
THE FAIRY TALE OF A HAPPY END
by Alexandra Berková
MEDICINE
by Piotr Sommer
TROBADORA BEATRIX
by Irmtraud Morgner
THE NIGHT OF THE BULGARIANS
by Henri Michaux

Francisco Segovia was born in Mexico City in 1958. Primarily a poet (El error *1981,* Triga *1984), he has also written essays* (Ocho notas *1985). These two pieces are from his recent short book of fictions, Conferencia de Vampiros, where the speakers elaborate on viruses, love and coincidence.*

Conference of Vampires

by Francisco Segovia

The Doctor's Explanation

I would like to have cultivated a genuine passion—for chess or cards, or some more solitary activity such as finding wise proverbs to illustrate the great Greek philosophers. Something profound and useless, like all the great passions. Instead I got interested in medicine.

This occurred many years ago, and in such a manner that it was hardly noticeable. At that time I barely even glimpsed the truth that the mediocrity of any profession whatsoever will, with the thick, slow crust of its assurance, compensate for any vice, especially that of enthusiasm. Thus I surrendered passion, and devoted myself instead to the cultivation of my craft. I was not idle in my study of classification and analysis, and still less so in the difficult subject of hygiene: so I easily learned the meticulous art of vaccination which I then practised for years with confident dexterity and a certain detachment. But even now I find it hard not to cross myself every time I observe—yes, with terror—a vaccine.

Whatever it is that makes me react so strangely, I'm certain that there is finally a very modern reason for it: the substitution in the preparation of vaccines of the noble and ancient bacillus by modern viruses. Let me explain.

Just as with any activity which can profitably be turned into a craft, vaccination has certain simple, essential rules to follow: the doctor must make sure his instruments are sterilized, prepared and arranged in one go so that they are to hand at all times and can be reached quickly in an emergency. Then proceed thus: with cotton soaked in alcohol clean the area of incision and pinch the skin where the needle will enter. Everything is then prepared for the inoculation of the bacillus, or the virus.

All this refers to the vaccination, strictly speaking, because the vaccine itself is nowadays far more complex. First you must catch the virus and keep it in its natural state while it is not being used. Part of the laboratory must be converted into a zoo where each specimen can be fed and where its survival—and indeed its reproduction, for that must be regarded as one of the conditions of its survival—can be guaranteed. This is the most complicated part of all, and it provokes the most disagreement and academic controversy, since the medical profession hasn't managed to come to any consensus on the nature of the natural state of the virus, or on what its real nature is; there isn't even any general agreement on where this extraordinary creation comes in the scale of evolution.

One thing is certain: a virus can produce

another virus, even though we don't know whether or not this process can properly be called reproduction. However, it seems clear that the functions of the virus are fairly elementary, and it seems probable that they can be reduced to just one: bite a cell and raise from its ruins a new virus.

The rest of the biology of this being (if it is indeed a being, with a biology of its own) belongs in the realm of metaphysical speculation. We do not know what it needs to survive, nor even if it absolutely needs anything at all. We neither know how it has come into existence, nor if it will cease to exist one day.

All this, as I explained, is a mystery. So much so that we doctors and biologists don't know what to think. Some researchers place the virus at the top of the evolutionary scale, others on the bottom rung. But what might mediate between these two extreme opinions covering the entire evolutonary scale isn't as serious a matter as the fact that they each use exactly the same arguments to come to completely opposed conclusions. In this way the virus is either the crown or the ruin of evolution, and could be either for exactly the same reasons. Like the love of God, the virus is without cause for the same reason that it is a necessity.

To sum up, we don't know if its functions and needs have been progressively reduced until it has become this prodigy of economy, or if, on the other hand, it has neither functions nor needs and has yet to take the first step on the long road of evolution. The entire mystery may be summed up in this statement, as clear as it is terrible: we do not know if the virus is alive or dead. And although we can prove that its bite produces a new virus in its own image and likeness, scientific method does not allow us to solve the mystery of the beginning and the end of this microscopic monster.

Although it is true that all this scientific ignorance confounds me and leaves me quite incapable of inoculating someone with such an unknown force, that isn't enough in itself to explain my terror or the helpless trembling of my fingers when I cross myself, as if I were standing in the presence of Evil. I explain it thus: in a being so reduced to one single and sole quality (to be neither living nor dead) and one single and sole activity (bite into and produce another, identical to itself) whatever resemblances there are resolve themselves necessarily into one single identity. Therefore, if we can find another elemental being with these qualities, we could be sure in what way such a new being is none other than the very same, identical virus. And we all know that elemental being is the vampire.

translated by Nick Drake

Francisco Segovia

The Tale of the Obsessive

In Romania the remedy against vampires is to scatter grains of millet on the body so that before leaving the grave they will have to count each one. The charm against the witch-vampires of Sardinia consists in leaving a dead cat or dog lying across the door of the house. Before entering, witches will spend hours counting each hair on the animal's body... They can then be trapped at sunrise.

Anthony Masters, A Natural History of the Vampire

I shouldn't say this, but perhaps it will lead to a better understanding of what I am about to relate: I am a lexicographer, an amateur in the world of books, and passionate about characters (not so much those in literature, but actual words and letters themselves). I love to track a word in the dust of a thousand others, searching for clues with absolute determination until finally I lose my way. I am possessed by an obsessive rage for the absolute which can lose men in the dusty shadows of the indefinable.

From my ancestors—dukes, counts, commoners—I inherited the never-ending habit of counting every last hair on the body of every cat I find at the entrance to a house. I have devoted myself to discovering something useful in this vicious enthusiasm; and I have managed to transform my ancestors' fascination into a philanthropic office: that of lexicography. Nevertheless, I have disturbed the neutrality of the ancient order: none of my predecessors even realized the significance of the word destiny. I, on the other hand, have learned to read its meaning in the most insignificant things, and now my mind and heart are completely possessed by their endless impertinence.

Theologists, learned men, teachers, butchers, street sweepers and others of our day agree on one thing: there are no longer any oracles. Although I am already a rather unusual creature —given the occupation and interests I have inherited from my ancient family—I am increasingly of the opposite view. I say that the thunderous voice of the universe can still be heard in the streets of the big cities, and that oracles have not ceased to speak; the infinite still speaks with an untied tongue, and does so now more freely than ever before. And for holding this opinion I have earned myself the alienation of my fellow men—if not complete incomprehension and sheer suspicion. I will briefly relate how this has come to pass.

Some years ago I had a girlfriend; she was very beautiful, with the rosiest cheeks. She was the first whose much-desired neck I learned to respect, despite having to endure instead a chaste, faithful diet of hens. But such a loyal and freely offered heart was not enough; she could not understand the patient labour of my abstinence, or supress the urgency of her first reproach. Inertia, with its eagerness for eternity, did the rest insatiably. So as not to answer her hot blood's desire with blood, I concentrated my mind on inner silence and darkness. In that mist of humility I found my girlfriend more pure, even abstract, and less provocative in the deliberate sparkling of flesh. So my security and her safety lay down there at the bottom of my bloodless heart. But outwardly, in the crowded world of the living, I seemed timid and timorous. Either way, I began to hate that pretend person, hated myself in the daylight world where I heard my girlfriend say, What's happened to you? These days you're not so self-assured...

I drive to forget. Since in my case alcohol and drugs are risky, and may even lead to fatal offences, I've learned to have nothing to do with them; instead I submerge myself in that ambiguous activity—a mixture of concentration and mechanical reflex—which is driving. Now you may say this is escapism and that it's nothing to be proud of. Agreed. But I've seen hens suffer less when confronted with death if they've been given a little Cognac to drink beforehand. The same happens with Christmas turkeys; a little escapism actually makes them more savoury than all the tough abnegation of the realists. I recognize that this culinary argument in favour of a moral position is more convenient for the diners than for the dish and that's why I'm making it, and not the chicken—but any sensible person would agree that it is not equally convenient for the escapists and for the realists.

The evening my girlfriend cruelly accused me of insecurity, I was driving the car, so I could pretend I hadn't heard her. I stared at the number plate of the car in front. It was from Puebla, or from Oaxaca, and had the following letters: IPT (I pity). Suddenly I heard my voice outside me saying, I pity. I pity you, my love.

I don't know if she heard this warning, but when we arrived at my house and I shut the door behind us, my ears were still buzzing. I threw myself onto her. I remember she howled, screamed, wept, tossed her lovely neck. Fainted.

But did anything like this really happen to her? No: rather, it all happened to me; the fury was satiated in my body, not hers. Nothing changed in the natural world.

I must add that I didn't love her so as to absorb her into my family. She didn't drink my blood, nor did she receive the vampire's baptism. My passion didn't have that ritual strictness which could have admitted her into my ancient family and ways. Instead I initiated her into something much greater and more secret: into that indifference I cannot know, and into which I cannot initiate myself, because it rejects me.

When I had satisfied the ancestral greed of my elders, I kissed her cold lips and left. I got into the car and drove into the city without thinking where I was heading. But the dark enthusiasm of the flesh had not been satisfied; and once more I heard my voice outside myself saying, All's well, my love, be just as you wish: now you know that world which is forever closed to me. Take from me that which I cannot receive from you. All's well, my love: dry. And I remembered her lying cold on the bed as I read a new number plate: DRY.

I stopped the car while I endured the barbaric echo of those terrible words. I lifted up my eyes in supplication: Gods of the Ancients, is this destiny? And before my eyes I saw TCS (Thesius) and the fearless EKT (Hecate). Can it be true? Can it be true?

To calm myself, I sank down into some sparse bushes in a park and stayed there away from the voices for several hours. Much later that night I emerged from my hiding place, prepared to confront the uproar. A hundred thousand demons were screaming in a confusion of voices. I began to make out—among lost messages, accusations, insults and crude advice—that they were mocking me: AGE (grow old), SIN (sin!), EKT PSS ONU (Hecate piss on you), YDR DRY (why dear, dry!), BST (beast). Reading the zero of a number plate as the letter "o", O BEY was... Obey.

The uproar wasn't useless though. I practised and perfected my reading until I understood that the first letters the oracle sent me (IPT) were not to be read as my own words, but as hers, so now she was echoing my voice: I pity... I pity you my love.

Towards dawn I was able to invoke my dead girlfriend. Since I wanted to avoid other voices interfering in our intimacy, I chose a sad, lonely, street to await her reply. My powers were fading with the night's darkness, and the approaching daylight sickened me. A car drew up beside me, and the driver asked for a light. I gave it to him hastily, hoping to see the miraculous number plate: it was an extraordinary message made up of an unusual combination of letters, including the abhorred cross on which my lovers had crucified me; it read IXU—I cross you; I bless you with the sign of the cross.

As he drove off, the driver could see I had fainted away. I gathered myself together and returned home. Since then I haven't ventured out. I've dedicated myself to a recondite lexicography and returned to the pious diet of hens. Since then I read everything, but in fear and in trembling.

translated by Nick Drake

STORM 7–8/1992

Luis Humberto Crosthwaite lives in the north of Mexico and was promptly recognized as a promising and unusual writer with the publication of this story. A Mexican woman with a hum-drum life comes slap-bang up against the personification of Americana: Elvis, on a seaside stroll. The King, now deposed, is disorientated and increasingly decrepit but the pair, outcast and misunderstood, fall in love and break hazily for the border.

Marcela and the King Together At Last on the Coast Path

by Luis Humberto Crosthwaite

Part One: Marcela

She had a cat, her only companion, but now she is alone again. Years, like the cat, have gone out of the window taking furniture and carpets with them.

The alarm clock goes off.

She gets up, washes and dresses. She takes the first bus to the centre and reaches work ahead of her colleagues. She takes her place facing the same desk, facing the same typewriter and facing the same tasks.

Eight hours later, she leaves and walks the same distance.

The same as ever.

No one greets her.

No one says, "Excuse me," to her.

Rock-and-roll has never touched her life.

That's the truth.

She has never reached out and touched it.

No one invites her to the café of an afternoon

or takes her dancing or to dinner or harvesting tomatoes on some Yankee farm across the border.

Her life had became a matter of one, two, three… (she gets up, washes, dresses…). She didn't understand there could be variations: one three two—two three one.

Marcela is forty and little by little (bye-bye Marcela) the wind is bringing her the sea inside.

You must see that a soap operas can be some solace when one of the characters is called Marcela and lives happily with her husband.

There was a time when Marcela understood people.

There was a phase when she walked along crowded streets and gave herself over to listening to the voices. Just listen—

"My brother went off with my cousin's wife…" "The Yanks are taking over Central America, the bastards…" "I can't leave the drunken cow… Cheers!" "That fellow has spent three weeks inside."

What do you think of that?

She understood everything.

It was the most constructive phase of her life, she thought.

To be understanding was ideal and educative but it didn't last long. The indifference of passers-by meant that they ceased to be of importance to her. No one said, "Excuse me," and she decided not to say it to anyone either.

So that was all right.

Due to this set of circumstances (Marcela perpetually in a bad mood), her sole companion chose the happy, reproductive life of an alley cat.

Amen. From time to time, contempt for people is also fine.

Just a phase, she'd say to the King soon after.

She was the last one onto the beach, before leaving the centre where people are colourless, and would sit down beside the ruins of the Coast Path.

She discovered that many of the people walking along it were like her. She got used to looking at them. Each had their own style and each was also identical.

To Marcela.

Good grief!

One day, she set eyes on the King for the first time.

PART TWO: THE KING

It's commonplace to come across the likes of Elvis on the border—vagabonds who drink, circle parks, sleep on benches or stretch out in front of liquor stores in the hope that either the police or oblivion will take them.

Whichever comes first.

Like it did for Jim Morrison, Janis Joplin, Jimmy Hendrix.

The figure of Elvis, fat and bejewelled, with rhinestone belt and rhinestone rings, suddenly appeared asking for directions to his penthouse in Las Vegas.

Poor guy, he had no idea it was all over.

"The End," said Jim Morrison, once upon a time.

Elvis approached a passer-by and said, "I've been so lonely. I've been so lonely I could die,"—but the fellow went on his way across Revolution Square.

Said nothing in reply.

Next Elvis spotted a traffic warden. He

shouted, "Oh let me be (oh let him be), your teddy bear."

The cop wasn't amused. In prison, the sorry gringo was stripped of the rhinestones decorating his outfit (in lieu of a fine) then thrown out on the street with a few pesos of change.

Elvis was in his forties and not overly concerned about work. He meant to find some, but it's hard on the border. There weren't many places that still offered live music: one among them, Mike's, had just signed up a rock singer. It's hard being broke.

"Sorry, mate."

The others weren't interested.

"You look too much like the King."

It was no good trying to explain.

He had the bright idea of singing on urban buses but was turfed off the first one. Passengers prefer children singing northern ballads to fat Larries singing rock-and-roll. What do they know about music? Then bad luck put him on route 11 to Los Pinos, whose passengers are the meanest of all.

Maybe on another route, who knows?

After this disappointment, Elvis stopped combing his hair and became grotesquely emaciated. His clothes hung off him in tatters, and thus attired (someone told him he had no alternative) he hung about and pestered young women who passed him on the Coast Path.

Again without success.

You and I know the King was born to sing.

Nothing else.

At that time, you could park your VW and see lots of guys like Elvis on the beach, ostracized for their appearance and their unpleasant smell, their long beards and greasy, curly locks. Either they'd be muttering to themselves or shouting aloud that they were the King, every one a different king.

How many times has this writer, sipping coconut milk beneath a giant sunshade, speculated on the question of who among them was the real King?

This was several years ago.

The Coast Path no longer exists.

What happened was that there was a storm that left the streets looking more chewed-up than a tuna sandwich, all the restaurants and pretty locations torn apart, worm-eaten like victims of time rather than the high tide with its waves and salt.

Corners without traffic lights.

Blocks without corners.

And no people.

Nobody likes the pathetic sight of the Coast Path any more. Now and again, a few bathers.

And Elvis walking alone, writing his name in the sand and watching it disappear among the foam and the seaweed—E L V I S.

Occasionally he would wander northwards until he reached the border.

The border has a large placard which reads,

HEY, YOU—BEWARE! YOU ARE ENTERING THE UNITED STATES OF AMERICA, THE MOST POWERFUL NATION IN THE WORLD! DON'T DO IT!

There were heroic days when the King dared to cross, but as soon as he was a few metres inside the border guards approached with their pistols at the ready.

Elvis no longer offered explanations, he felt

too alone. He wrote, "Love me tender, love me sweet," in the sand and returned, full of sorrow.

Once, Elvis walked into the sea and waited a long while in the waters of the Pacific. The waves rose and fell like a Carlos Santana guitar riff, lament of the earth, smile of the sun. When he emerged, he still looked unpleasant but he smelt like a fishing port, sweet to this writer, irksome to others.

A woman spent her time gazing at him with neither sadness or joy. They were the only people on the beach. The sun came a few millimetres closer.

"I am the King. My name is Elvis."

Strangely, she seemed to understand.

PART THREE: THE BORDER

The King spoke emotionally with Marcela about Buddy Holly, Priscilla, and rhythmic movements that can make any hip ripple (he didn't say "pelvis"); about his drug addiction, about how to win at black jack in certain casinos in Las Vegas and about the border.

Pausing a while north of the border he told her, "That's it," pointing out the placard.

Marcela told him about her work, her old, ungrateful cat, overtime and taxes. She also gave him a crash course in shorthand, using the sand as a giant whiteboard.

They fell in love at once.

Marcela was uninterested in the fact that Elvis was divorced. They wandered northwards, chatting, until they came up against the placard (HEY, YOU... etc). Marcela said that close to, it wasn't as big as it seemed from a distance.

That was how she, having nothing better to do, decided to cross the famous boundary they call "The Frontier", otherwise known as a row of little crosses on every map which we're indoctrinated to respect from primary school on.

The King did the same.

They both began their journey along the beach, with no destination in mind.

Soon the guards arrived.

PART FOUR: THE LAST

Marcela and Elvis, together at last.

The others, the idiots, shouted, "STOP!"

Helicopters arrived and shone their most powerful spotlights on the pair. Elvis felt like he was on stage.

Journalists arrived, and television cameras, as the two of them continued walking and the placard receded into the distance, so diminutive that it seemed about to disappear.

The guards started to shoot.

But what use are bullets?

Marcela and Elvis kept on walking. She received rock-and-roll for the first time. He sang hits of yesteryear beneath the intense beam of the helicopters.

This was a lot better than it had ever been in Las Vegas.

Those morons never understood that neither they nor their pistols existed for Marcela and the King who were, like the border, just little crosses on a map burnt to cinders long ago.

translated by Amanda Hopkinson

Carmen Boullosa, was born in Mexico City in 1954. She has worked in the theatre and written plays (13 señoritas *1983,* Xe Bubulú *1984,* Cocinar hombres *1985,* Los totoles *1985) and poetry* (El hil olvida *1978,* La memoria vacía *1978,* Ingobernable *1979,* La voz y Método completo de recreo sin acompañamiento *1983) as well as novels* (La Midas *1986,* Mejor desaparece *1987) and owns a theatre bar in Coyoacan.*

They're Cows, We're Pigs, a novel from which this is an extract, is set among seventeenth-century pirates. Boullosa explores the extremes of male brutality and the frightening edges of lawlessness in a shocking antidote to picturesque notions of freedom on the high seas. Here, "cows" is the pirates' phrase for land-lubbers, those who have settled down, who live in houses, grow vegetables, obey laws. "Pigs" are the buccaneers, free men who roam the free world robbing, looting, raping, drinking—and answering to no man.

The story so far: Jean Smeeks, a poor orphan from Flanders, ran away to sea and found himself ship-wrecked on Tortuga Island. Accustomed to cruelty and deprivation, he was twice treated kindly: once by the freed slave, Black Honey, who taught him herbalism, and once by Pineau, a surgeon who instructed him in his trade. As we join him, both have been murdered and Smeeks, obsessed with avenging their deaths, has signed up as a doctor on a pirate ship. He writes a log book to keep alive the memory of his mentors, recording in it the adventures of the buccaneers.

They're Cows We're Pigs

by Carmen Boullosa

Two months. Eight weeks. Sixty days. How many hours? Disembarking on the island of Aruba in the Gulf of Mexico for the boatswain to organize the distribution of the plunder and for L'Olonnais to make a safe reconnoitre of Tortuga Island and my chance to redeem myself at the head of the assault on Maracaibo. It had all begun with the siege on the castle conducted at such a lick that, to tell the truth, the canoe I was travelling in hadn't touched dry land before we buccaneers were already the victors and the Spaniards already the vanquished. This proved to be the first occasion on which the buccaneers called on my surgical skills. I removed several impacted bullets—one from a thigh, another from an arm, three more from shoulders before tending to the stab wounds...We entered the city without a fight. A few days later I cut off one of my fingers and noted its loss in the logbook I had to hand over to the boatswain for him to organize the distribution of the booty at the expedition's end. At Aruba, before handing over the catalogue of arms, fingers, eyes and other missing limbs, I went over the list again: one leg had been blown away by cannon fire and I simply tied the arteries; a second had had to be amputated, because it had arrived along with its buccaneer, fractured and burnt by a gunpowder explosion.

I ran my eyes down the list and was able to recreate the deeds of the assault, yet something still eluded my understanding. That period of time, those sixty days, had brought me to bay. I was no longer myself now the Trepaner had become master of my actions. In my log-books, which I had now to produce, I'd recorded eighty-four severed legs, and privately I was unsure of how to count the Church images we'd blasphemed, the Spanish women we'd raped, the meals we'd consumed in lavish mansions, the tortures I'd witnessed... How long was it since I had been press-ganged, enslaved, how long since I'd slept in the fresh air on the verandah of the house where I grew up and from whence I was expelled? I was incapable of writing up the assault on Maracaibo after our return. I was no longer a person, I had become no more than a fist which brandished a sword that haemorrhaged blood, an eye which took aim, a finger which squeezed a trigger. I was the bodies of those we'd killed—with or without a reason—when they got in the way of our seizing the fruits of their labour for our pleasure, or for the delight of watching them die, of hearing their bodies fall, of splashing ourselves with their Spanish blood... And I was the bodies I had healed, into which

I'd inserted my scalpel, my blade, my knife...

Yet was I really no more than this? Were not my forefathers Black Honey and Pineau, who instilled in me the secrets of nobility and grandeur? At long last I was now a Brother like the rest of them, of the Secret Brotherhood of Coastal Brethren. That way I shared the sweetest dream of those two good men, whose honour was stained up to the elbows with the blood now dripping from my hands... No, I was unable to recreate myself. But within my body I felt such a sense of satisfaction that it almost dulled my sense of adventure, my joy in buccaneering. Was I lost? In thus questioning myself, I knew that I had only lost my body, that I'd been no more than a slave, a conscript, and that on ceasing to be that I'd merely become a slave whose body was no longer his own...

I couldn't understand any of it. I couldn't understand why, among buccaneers, there was such a preference for taking women by force rather than using the whores. Least of all did I understand what the point was in selecting Spanish women for whom rape spelt such utter degradation, who fought back so fiercely and then lived out the humiliation of their defeat so dolorously? How, most of all, Spanish virgins fight to preserve their honour!—for once we've used them they lose all hope of making a good match, and rather than see themselves unsuitably married off to someone of low estate, an old buffer, a widower or a fellow endowed with some hideous defect, they'd sometimes prefer to assume the mantle of martyrdom.

In Gibraltar a young girl and her mother still possessed of good looks clung on, defenceless, in their home when the city fell. The mother was mindful of the pirates' reputation for gross excess and immediately sent her servant to fetch in prostitutes and her cooks to prepare food, leaving a note which read as follows:

Our brave men have been vanquished. This house surrenders as did they. Everything here is yours, the house and all it contains, you have conquered. I have had women brought here to afford you the pleasures to which you are said to be so attached. I am a woman of honour and my daughter is but a girl. We make this one appeal to your feelings (assuming you have any), and beg to be treated with respect.

—The Marchioness of Poza Rica

As this was one of the two grandest mansions in the city, it was immediately seized by the buccaneers and we were received there like real gentlemen, fêted with food and drink, females and every other kind of convenience, a truly magnificent feast at which we were accorded every formality. When L'Olonnais, seated at the head of the table, enquired to whom they might be indebted for such a good reception, a servant brought him the note written by the good lady. He had barely finished reading it before he ordered a thorough search, adding, "You are not to remove anything from these premises for it's of no interest to us what gets fed to the cows if there are still two jewels here with which to adorn ourselves, buccaneers!" The servants and whores attempted to convince us otherwise but only succeeded, by their very reasoning and insistence, in delaying the search and earning their own executions.

The house was turned over from top to bottom. A youngster was grotesquely maltreated to extract information as to the whereabouts of his mistress but the torture was wasted since before a word passed his lips death took him, preceded by violation, castration and a flaying alive that robbed him of strips of his skin. Someone had the idea of torching the house but was dismissed by the captain saying, "These idiots prefer death in flames to surrendering in our arms."

By chance, their hiding-place was revealed. On the second floor, while three of us at a time were taking turns to jump and pull down a ceiling canopy behind which we imagined they might lie concealed, our boots went through a wooden joist to the floor below. Looking down, one of us caught the glint of an eye crossing a ray of sunlight directed downwards by the shard of a treacherous, fallen mirror. On lifting the floor, we discovered our two beauties and amid raucous jokes, banter and gropes from those they had attempted to elude, the women were brought before the Admiral. We all stared at them lasciviously—how true it was that here were two pearls, the mother in her maturity, the girl in the freshness of youth.

The mother addressed L'Olonnais in Spanish then, since he paid her no attention assuming, that he couldn't understand her, switched to French, which she spoke with a perfect accent and touching manner, "Admiral, we recognize you as our victor, and offer you all that is within this house. I personally arranged your reception, concerning which you can have no complaints. Since I know you are a gentleman I make only one solitary plea, that you should respect my person as that of an honourable woman who has known no other man but my husband, and that of my daughter, my greatest treasure, who as you see is merely a child. I beseech you again, although this house is no longer as well, ordered" (this, on looking around at the havoc wreaked by our search) "as you deserve for your reception."

"Marchioness, we are not cows and we don't subsist on mud and grass without enjoying the jewels to be found among them too. As you yourself say in your note, you two are the greatest pearls to be found in this house. We have no interest in touching anything here, not even the safes of money we have discovered in our searches, nor the silver plate, nor the supplies. All we intend to take are the two pearls."

"Captain, I beg you. Take me if you will but spare my daughter, I beseech you."

"Woman, be still. L'Olonnais is infuriated by pleading and irritated by supplication. It is not for you to give me orders, you a vanquished woman and a Spaniard...!"

There was scant further dialogue before the women, seeing the evidence of their defeat in the fact that the men were already lifting up their skirts with their swords and slitting their corsets with the tips of their blades, attempted to flee; in the midst of the uproar, right there before the rest of us and the lady of the house, L'Olonnais seized the daughter and another seized the mother, followed by who knows how many more in a like performance, each one in front of the others, and when the gang was done they summoned more buccaneers to abuse the wonen and so many came that when we left them—and I saw this with my own eyes—the women were torn and broken, bleeding everywhere like live meat, with wounds surrounding their genitals. When we finally left, mother and daughter together set fire to their home, the necessary strength drawn from I know not where. I've no idea how they could even gather themselves up from the floor (still less how one of them could call out, over and over, who knows which of the two was driven mad enough to keep repeating "Go on, pirate, enjoy it! Enjoy it, pirate! Enjoy it, pirate!") and there they died, the very day we violated them, when we buccaneers transformed them from damsels into whores and from whores into raw meat.

It took us two months to mount the assault of Maracaibo. Within four days we were counting the booty on Aruba and weighing anchor to distribute the loot, which had to be done first on paper, since before landing on the Spanish island of Tortuga we needed to pause and sell the merchandise at the port called Isle of Cows. Together with the boatswain L'Olonnais, the expedition's surgeon (myself), and some seventy from among the bravest, we all set sail a day ahead of the rest of the fleet on board a sloop, the lightest boat of the lot, without any of the booty but well supplied with victuals to resume our route to Hispaniola and, should it be necessary in case of an intended ambush, clear it of any enemies.

Shortly after we'd left our companions, the lookout announced the sighting of a boat, possibly a warship sent in search of us. We rapidly approached and got her on our tail, to draw her away from Aruba and the plunder we'd left there with some of our men, then headed for the end of the isle furthest from our point of departure. When we reached dry land it was already nightfall and, although we'd left the Spaniards behind us, the island wasn't large enough to remove the risk of our men being hunted down, should they lose track of us. We dropped anchor and disembarked in Indian canoes with the artillery. Our days were spent in the interior, hiding ourselves and our cannon in the thickest woodland, in a twilight saved from black-out by the moon painting the sky blue and the branches a deep grey, even though it was not yet full and so didn't shine too brightly.

The woodland dwellers did not appear to be intimidated by our presence. We heard their faint movements along with those of the leaves and branches, sometimes scraping the rough bark of the trees as they slid to the sand or slithered on the smooth stones—although I'm aware that so many words seem to exaggerate the miniscule movements we noticed, like animals moving in their sleep, in their dreams, as if our arrival hadn't even awoken them. I, like many other buccaneers, feared the alligators, so had taken a dog along for company at Maracaibo, but this time I got orders to leave him on board, locked into an empty hold, where we already knew he felt at home and would be kept too busy by the rats to start barking—or that if he did bark, no one would hear him. The official orders were right: the whispers of the wood would indeed have made him nervous and he'd have barked so loudly that although I'd have brought him along to calm my nerves, he'd have had my heart turn somersaults.

The Spanish frigate silently slipped towards the coast, believing us to be asleep, since our sloop gave no indication of our being awake. Scarcely had it approached close enough than we attacked with our heavy artillery, taking it by surprise in the twilight, overcoming its superior strength in the confusion of not knowing whether to fire at our ship, at the canoes which by then had also been spotted, or at the sky. It never entered their Spanish heads that buccaneers might attack from under cover of woodland and weeds.

We won, as was to be expected, and amid the screeching retorts of dawn in the Antilles, L'Olonnais accepted the enemy's surrender, without them knowing—until too late—the terms of their rout: that within the hour, or whatever other time he named, L'Olonnais would put them all to the sword: from the most senior General down to the last in line, from Captain Don Pedro de Avellaneda, to the Commander-in-Chief of the Army and Master of the Land Forces, Don Gónzalo Suárez Ossiz; from the Sergeant Major and Captain of one of the Companies to the Battalion Commander; from the Artillery Commander down to the assistants, midshipmen, chaplains, holders of royal offices, the commissary for provisions and the quartermaster...

Our sloop was damaged, and we found ourselves obliged to seize the frigate even though it was poorly suited for the return voyage of our expedition. We sent a canoe round the island to warn our companions of the change of plan, and waited for it to return to avoid proceeding with a reduced number of men and resources. We then threw overboard the surplus weight carried aboard the frigate, save only the meagre stores that was all our gain, and mounted our cannon.

When the canoe returned it brought a boy who had been caught red-handed. A Brother had clasped him in his embrace only to feel a hard object hidden in his belt. He demanded to see it and since the boy was his fag, he was obliged to obey and show it to him: it turned out to be a heavy necklace of gold and rubies the sailor boy had come across somewhere in Maracaibo and failed to hand over to the Brethren for their just and fair distribution of the booty. L'Olonnais had the thief brought before him. In front of us all he sliced off the swindler's nose and ears. I cooled the wounds with herbs given me by Black Honey. We brought him on board the frigate, and when we set sail we abandoned him on an islet with a wineskin of water and a musket and bullets for his only companions. I wish he'd have made good use of them, the scoundrel, to blow his brains out instead of embarking on the protracted agony that precedes death in the midst of an immense sea when a high tide swept over the tiny plot of land on which he stood! No one felt the least sympathy for the sailor who so richly deserved his fate.

Without further interruption and within the week we reached the Isle of Cows, a port where a group of French freebooters had settled and sold dried meat to buccaneers and traders who visited there intending to do business with them.

We unloaded what we'd looted, including the statues and paintings and even the bells from Maracaibo church—and the five hundred cows. We divided these female prisoners amongst us, according to the terms of our contract. Having done the accounts, we found the loose change amounted to two hundred and sixty thousand pieces of eight. Once distributed, we each received lengths of silk, linen, and other items to the value of over a hundred pieces of eight. The wounded, beginning with the mutilated, obtained their share first of all: for the loss of a right arm, six hundred pesos or six slaves; for a left arm, five hundred pesos or five slaves; for a right leg, five hundred pesos or five slaves; for a left leg, four hundred pesos or four slaves; for an eye, a hundred pesos or a slave; for a finger the same as for an eye...

Afterwards, all the engraved plate was weighed and valued at ten pieces of eight a pound. The jewellery was divided according to variable estimates, given our complete ignorance on its real worth. We moved on to the division of the shares of those who'd died in battle or through other misadventure. Their portions were given into the care of their friends to be passed on, when the time came, to their beneficiaries.

Once the distribution was over we set sail for Tortuga Island, reaching it a month after calling in at the Isle of Cows, to the great joy of those we'd left behind who were running out of money. When we got to Tortuga the traders were already waiting for us. And the whores. And the innkeepers. And the gaming house owners. And every kind of creature who expected to fleece us at the feast.

The night that had begun on my previous visit to Jamaica followed me to Tortuga and still wasn't over.

No complaints, our nights were given over to merriment. Our men arrived close behind the two ships laden with wine and spirits plundered by other buccaneers, sold in Jamaica and transported to Tortuga. The first day, alcohol came as cheap as sun or pasture on those islands. Ten days later it was worth ten times more; another ten days and it had increased in value a hundredfold, changing its worth from grass to gold, although it was continually converted into

STORM 4:

"...Continues to impress with an unusual blend of writers and nationalities. This is new, sometimes bizarre writing at its best, a refreshing antidote to the effects of reading too much comfortable, mainstream stuff."
Scotland on Sunday

DIXIE CHICKEN
by Kate Sterns
TIAMAT
by Urszula Benka
CROATIAN FULL MOON AND OTHER POEMS
by Drago Stambuk
NIGHT BLINDNESS
by Undine Gruenter
THE DEATH OF DJUNA BARNES
by Ewa Kuryluk
MANSTER
by Rick Moody
INTERIOR WITH SNOW
by Geneviève Serreau
THE SINISTRA NATURAL HISTORY COLLECTION
by Adám Bodor

another substance as it ran down our throats: at first it lived like a golden sun in our bodies, suffusing us with the light of a candle-stub flaring its last, an artificial and flickering light across the dark fiesta. As it spent the succeeding days inside us it became a hard, grey stone, almost black deep within us, in our guts, our blood, our muscles, darkening more and more, as though acclimatizing us to the enveloping night.

We became all too acclimatized in the succeeding days to gambling at table, to placing high stakes and paying high prices to use the chips and the counters. The musicians who accompanied us in our assaults now fell silent, though others went on to lighter tunes and wherever you went you could hear them. It seemed to me they never stopped playing the entire night, for I never ceased hearing them. Now and then you could also hear the strange music of the negro slaves.

The La Casa women travelled to Port Royal to keep us company. They had created a piece of theatre for our reception. When the curtains were drawn, we were presented with tableaux vivants perfectly created in every detail. Among the buccaneers there were some who recognized famous paintings in the scenes thus depicted, some who considered their reproduction perfect, above all Vouet's *Death of Dido*, which won the greatest admiration. It was said that it was so resplendent because Dido was really the Madame (as I remember her, just a slip of a girl), and Vouet's lover. I could swear that one of the tableaux was identical to one we'd robbed. We laughed at the idea of the paintings from the walls of Maracaibo church exciting the fervour of Spanish breasts as we saw the Virgin modelled by one of our prostitutes, a St Joseph by the girl's pimp, even St Anne by the girl we'd taken turns with the other night, and the infant Jesus in his crib looking like a hen about to lay... When the display was over, under the beautiful pavilions they'd set out among the rocks and trees, the women surrendered themselves to the satisfaction of our carnal appetites.

We tasted and ate sumptuously of dishes that seemed prepared by fairies and witches, giving a heart to our bodies and a body to our hearts in a manner denied the whores themselves.

Van Wijn, the dealer, took the cards. He shuffled the three decks together. He got Foothunter, sitting on his left, to cut them and called for ten pieces of eight. The Tunisian, on his right, called a ducat real, and one ducat after another, they reached the ten Van Wijn wanted to open with. He turned over a card, the dealer's; it was the three of clubs. Then without hesitation, a second card to the left of his own, one belonging to the punters. It was the ace of hearts. Straight away he turned over another card and the men began loudly refusing to play either with the dealer's or the punters' cards. Another card was turned over. The punters called out, "Ace of hearts! Ace of hearts!", yelling and gesticulating. The scene was like a barnyard. Like pigs when the buccaneers come in for supplies for their voyages, whether their owners like it or not, the beatings will change their minds for them! Barnyards so full of pigs, so packed with pigs that the pigs are unable even to move. They kept on squealing, "Deal again! Three of clubs!" The dealer Van Wijn won.

He shuffles once more. Foothunter cuts. He

calls, "Thirty pieces of eight." The Tunisian replies, "Three ducats," and lays them on the card table, followed in turn by nine other players. He turns up a seven of clubs. The barnyard is in uproar: the card is a sign of bad luck. The dealer throws down an ace of hearts for the punters. The next card after those two is another ace of hearts. The dealer loses.

He retires from the game, but before going settles his account with Benazet, a Frenchman, who grows richer by the day through renting out games at the buccaneers' expense. As on Tortuga Island, there is no one to referee the game and no taxes to pay. He hands a fixed sum over to the governor and rakes in the money. He doesn't drink. He doesn't keep a woman and women don't matter to him; he doesn't have to pay to maintain them or for them to support themselves. He doesn't enjoy food. He doesn't pay the musicians who play in the gambling den. Whenever he's the dealer he wins. The only luxury in his place is a decorated sign hung with flowers and vases that reads, THE GAME AWARDS EVERY PLEASURE SURPRISE CAN BRING —BARON DE MONTESQUIEU. An army of slaves tend the lands around the gaming house, growing tobacco that they dry before folding the leaves on their laps to sell for their weight in gold. They say it's the best tobacco. Land on Tortuga is the property of no man. Benazet simply exploits it without having to pay for doing so.

Benazet called me aside. He threatened me over something I couldn't understand. I hadn't been playing today, nor drinking. I'd spent the morning teaching two of the lads how to apply bandages. But I'd also spent time taking note of how good Benazet was in getting the others to lose in his favour. He threatened me again. And again. I couldn't grasp what he was on about. Every time he raised his voice a little more. The punters, the banker, the players, all lifted their eyes from the game to watch what was going to happen. He shouted even more loudly at me: he hadn't noticed that everyone was looking at him. I couldn't follow his argument—my attention was on watching what they were looking at, observing the Brethren's faces and Benazet's blossoming rage, a rage I'd never imagined such a stingy person could muster. He continued threatening me repeatedly, then let fall a name that hit me like a dull thud on the nose: Pineau. My eyes misted over. Blood was pounding in my ears. My legs wanted to leap but refused to obey even themselves.

I was not the only one to react so strongly to that name. Behind the rush of blood clouding my senses, somehow I was still aware of falling chairs, tumbling dice, flying blows... Not the shouts nor the talk nor the mutterings nor the contained barnyard turbulence that there'd been during the game. The gaters had been opened and the animals were scattered abroad.

All of us against Benazet and his men, who clearly preferred flight to continuing as his bodyguards. All the Brethren against Benazet.

When it was over, I saw Benazet curled up on the mud floor of his gambling den. Literally mashed to bits. The Brethren embraced me one by one. In total silence.

I burst into tears, as they continued taking it in turns to hug me. One brought me a glass of sweet wine to diminish my pain and said, "Now we've done for him. He won't kill you as he killed him. You don't have to be afraid of any of them. They're cows."

There, stretched out dead in front of me, lay Pineau's murderer.

The wine rising in my blood, I stood on his broken body and stamped, losing all sense of time, until there was nothing but a suppurating dough beneath my heels, like a mess of vomit, of stew, with the clothes ripped to shreds, little bits of bread floating in a thick corn soup: I was the Trepaner and that mess was the murderer of the two men who had made me who I am.

As I gave vent to my fury, leeching my pain out through my heels, most of the brothers returned to their gaming and a small group hunted about for the place where Benazet kept his ducats concealed. Once discovered, they were handed over to Antonio Du Puis, master of the expedition to Maracaibo, for him to add to the plunder to be distributed amongst us. This prolonged the feasting, on which a special ray of sunshine beamed thanks to the vengeance of Benazet's death, the death of that Frenchman who was never anything more than the filth we made of him.

This was my revenge, although I still didn't understand how Pineau and Black Honey had died at the hands of the mean and unscrupulous Benazet. This was my revenge but, even though my heart gave vent to it then, it still failed to sink into my understanding. Even now, despite all this, I recall these events in order to revive the memory of Black Honey, I can feel that slippery dough into which Benazet—the shit—was turned by the blows of the Brethren and the trampling of my uncontrollable feet. How strangely this dough, brought back to beneath my heels by memory, does nothing to upset my balance or sense of stability. On the contrary, thanks to its memory I tread more firmly, more surely, and the smell of farewell makes the blood that no longer freely circulates through my veins run more back towards those lengthened days, all turned to night ever since I signed my allegiance to the Law of the Coast.

The next item we sold to support our life of extravagance was a ship laden with cocoa. The thrifty purchaser was the governor, who gave for it only a twentieth part of its value.

The moment had finally arrived for us Coastal Brethren to open our purses in support of one another. We didn't need to look at each other to know what was going on all around us: the Las Casas women dismantled the pavilions and set off home to Jamaica; the traders circled about us, offering coppers for objects of great magnificence; the improvised dancing halls spread with succulent banquets evaporated into thin air… Before being bled completely white, those of us with still a few coins generously shared them out with the rest, according to good buccaneering tradition. Or so it always was until the arrival of the Second Fifty began.

The First Fifty were the Spaniards, a flexible assault troop composed of fifty men divided into detachments who kept criss-crossing the woods of Santo Domingo to surprise and attack the freebooters in their lairs. Between one fifty and the next, they succeeded in routing the rough freebooters from the north of the island.

The Second Fifty arrived on Tortuga and was as big a disgrace as the first. Luckily for us they were not made up of fifty-times-fifty but of a single fifty, although it was as damaging to the

Coastal Brethren as the first had been to the freebooters.

Yet the reader must be warned: if I restricted myself to recounting how this Second Fifty arrived, the havoc they wreaked on Tortuga, its sudden demise and the discovery these events brought me concerning Pineau and Black Honey, this story would not be over. If instead I return to it again and again, it's only to fulfil the promise I made to Black on his death-bed, charging me with the perpetuation of his memory. And I want to continue the story of cruel L'Olonnais, so as not to leave him still hanging on, and relate to you how the death he so richly deserved came about. Nor do I want to leave you, my readers, picturing us evermore on those turbulent seas. Better to return to Europe whence today (if indeed from anywhere) I bring you this tale.

But to return to where we'd reached in our story: when there was no longer a single one among us with a cent to contribute to the feasting, we spurred L'Olonnais on to mounting another inspired assault. While it was taking place some left in canoes to attack the turtle-fishers; others set out to try their luck at sea (they said that with considerable ill-fortune the moment came in which those dying of hunger attacked the humble inhabitants of the coast simply in order to seize their cassava-flour and dried fish; their hunger was so great that at times the destitute residents were able to throw our men out of their homes without surrendering anything); still more went to Hispaniola to obtain a sufficiency of provisions and the rest went careening off, some with the ships still belonging to L'Olonnais, chafing to depart on the next expedition.

When Caribs prepare to go to war, they throw *aji* onto burning coals. This spicy hot chilli thereby provokes a sinal irritation and a rasping cough which, they hope, induces the state of mind necessary to mount a furious attack. We, the buccaneers, have recourse neither to *aji* or chilli pepper, nor do we feign the frenzies of those who do in order to get ready to do battle with the Caribs. We find the energy for our buccaneering attacks in our empty pockets, our dry throats, our weariness with gorging on food and wine for weeks on end, and our satiation with the prostitutes, those women of such different aspect to ourselves who shared and put up with our explosive spirits (whenever they occurred) to achieve something approaching peace induced by alcohol, gaming, over-eating and music. Women who were in luck if a client paid up without haggling and scheming for the services of their profession. As I have said before, buccaneers prefer to take their women by force, finding enjoyment in humiliating those who resist and pleasure in extreme violence. One buccaneer (whose name I shall keep silent so that his soul, surely in agony, will not seek out vengeance against me) liked to kill the woman he was using, saying that dying flesh so increased his excitement that there could be no greater delight than putting a woman thus used to death. There were a great number who followed his recommendation in order to corroborate it, some who confirmed its veracity and others who denied it, while the rest found distinct pleasures in the possessing and in the killing.

Who, knowing the nature of our indulgences, could be surprised at the character of our assaults and combats? Who, knowing of these, could believe we needed any kind of *ají* prepared on burning coals to inflame our ardour? And who, knowing all of this, could fail to comprehend that among such men there could be a gradual change of feeling and sensations, depending on what took place before the battle, after or during an attack, whether the plunder was safely in the bag or hopelessly squandered...

Even for an instant, what with the shock of the memory of Pineau and Black Honey being revived by that shit Benazet's threats and his death, and the business of preparing my surgical equipment for the next expedition, since our departure seemed imminent, I had to distance myself from such extreme emotions, from that body of men formed by the buccaneers as a warm and ready whole, now I could well understand how as buccaneers we were also desperadoes. What could we do on dry land, with empty pockets, if we couldn't manage to quell the incursions of those who restlessly combed the coastal waters? When, at midnight, overcome by alcohol and with it coursing in our veins, we were irresistibly awoken to wonder how men could live on dry land, enclosed within four walls; how could they withstand the call of the roseate evenings in the New World; how indeed, without the calming effect of the open seas, of water without end, without corners, without banks, without ports...? Because whether on the high seas or destroying what the rest of mankind built to block it out, our buccaneering hearts would find a place to stay the drunken flow of blood coursing through our veins!

Before we could stem the fever engendered

by our siege of the city, before we could set it aside and regard it as a thing apart from ourselves, before we could further learn to convince ourselves that the battle was over, that we'd made ourselves rich, before any of that—we found that we had not a cent to call our own, not a shirt on our backs, nor lengths of silk, linen or rough homespun... We didn't realize that our story's end had already arrived before we were again precipitated into another attack. Every afternoon, then, we raised the red siege banner, and every dawn the flag fluttered enormous before our eyes, and although others may have been unaware of the significance of its scarlet hue enveloping the rich colours of the Caribbean, we knew that it was a battle cry, that for buccaneers it was a call to continue fighting and destroying, that our mission was in no sense over, that we had to struggle on with a musket in each hand, daggers between our teeth, albeit out of step, out of time, suffering constant delays, when the only thing we could count on was that beyond the stupefied black wrath induced by alcohol, however submerged a buccaneer may become in it, he can never forget that, before all else, he is one of the Coastal Brethren.

As Mansvelt discovered at the siege of Santiago, city of the hinterland. When the city was taken, when the buccaneers had wrested all its wealth, they set to feasting in that selfsame Santiago, sharing their triumph with the defeated inhabitants. They got the lot of them drunk, the old folk and the youths, even the children, forcing them to drink from the vast kegs manufactured for market. Then the drunken and defeated city was obliged to make the wealthy dance for the amusement of the poor inhabitants, for whom the fine señoritas were also put on display, their dresses ripped open, drunk and shouting, available to all. They tore the buttons from the trousers of the governor—from whom they'd already received a ransom—who blundered drunkenly to and fro, yelling in a vain attempt to impose order, his breeches halfway to his knees, stammering words he could no longer form due to the quantity of alcohol that had been forcibly tipped down his throat.

Halfway through the drunken orgy, the buccaneers undertook the exodus of considerable loads of plunder, taking it onto the beaches where they'd beached their boats. There a group of sober citizens under the command of the inebriate governor attempted to detain them, and might have succeeded had it not it been for Mansvelt and his brothers, floating on a haze of rum that clouded their actions, still reliving the stage in the battle when, taking stock of their military strength and equipment, they had devised how to make Santiago theirs. They confronted the Spaniards, seized the governor once more, each gang firing on the other until all ammunition was exhausted and they all fell silent. They then launched into every imaginable vituperation, the buccaneers demanding a fresh ransom for the governor, concerning whom no answer came. The Spaniards, bored with the war of words, had withdrawn.

Mansvelt and his men—without really knowing whether at the time of the attack or the feasting or the latter assault, their nerves as stretched as those of any true buccaneer worth his salt—headed for the quay, boarded the ships and, at the point of departure, received a miserly sum for the governor's second ransom. Never was a governor worse paid or worse attired, his breeches dropping stubbornly floorwards! So, although Mansvelt might desperately persist in celebrating his victory ahead of time, in keeping with his buccaneer's blood, they couldn't deny him his celebration, however they might detain him on grounds of inebriation. Drunk as he was, he fought like a wild animal, and by his lights there was no inebiration, no enibriation, no inobriatian, no inebriation, and above all no intoxication, acting like Rackham, a pirate but no buccaneer, who could lose his ship in an English attack, he and all his gang hopelessly intoxicated though struggling to safeguard two women—the rich and wilful Anne Bonny, and the poor and keen-witted Mary Read, before she became a pirate. We then had no reason to settle things through the Coastal Brethren, since all this occurred after we had dissolved our band, when Esquelín had been dead thirty years—when Port Royal, a port of pleasing magnificence, was still beaten by the tides, but why not say as much here, if our slow buccaneering conscience can be as swift as our reactions, when located outside time...?

Our spirits inflamed, our bodies but matter yearning for gold and in that sense but dead flesh, we buccaneers prepared ourselves for the following attack.

It was night when we realized we had become separated from the rest of the ships. Did this already denote a lack of expertise? Were the winds foretelling what would follow? Better for them if the hurricane were unleashed before reaching us! Better to be swallowed by the waves of the sea, caught in the narrow coves of the island of Guadalupe, a sea entry surrounded by high reefs, onto which they were helplessly driven by a current they had wrongly assumed to be kindly!

We had left in search of canoes, on board a sloop. This was because L'Olonnais had determined the spot for the next assault and because the waters there were shallow, we had to make use of canoes. These we intended to seize from the turtle-fishers, even though they were never armed and their canoes were their most prized possessions. It was an unpleasant task and one I'm still uncertain how I got involved in it. The rest of the buccaneers waited for us on Tortuga Island.

"Ship ahoy!"

The boatswain gave the order to bring our boat alongside the Spanish galley, flagging it down with the red banner that signalled their surrender. In the wink of an eye we would be on board the heavy ship with its strange crew: the archbishop was arguing vehemently with the captain, refusing to listen to reason; the officers issued contradictory orders to left and right; the second-in-command was struck dumb with panic. The archbishop, with little notion of the kind of men we were, urged for battle with the buccaneers in order to prevent the men from fleeing into the interior, abandoning all else but saving their skins as the captain wanted. I know not whether this was a cowardly or a wise course of action, for although they were well supplied with stores and ammunition the fellow knew they were lost and the soldiers set to guard the archbishop and his riches, instead of preparing themselves with caution and ardour for the wild battle which was upon them, began a loud lamentation on finding themselves separated from the rest of the fleet. Meanwhile the galley slaves, deaf to the confusion of orders, rowed on slowly, lacking any coordination, leaving the boat to weave about clumsily, almost grotesquely, and without direction.

As soon as we approached closely enough to view the deck, the musicians broke into dissonant playing at full volume. At the sound of the cacophony everyone began dancing on the hatches, the captain in his outworn gold-braided doublet, narrow silk breeches and hat adorned with broken plumes. To keep him company we all shook our jewellery and our legs, waved our arms from side to side, and fired our weapons into the air. There we were, still dancing, when the two prows met, crashing against each other, still with our muskets in our hands and our daggers between our teeth. Having thus holed our own sloop in order to have no means of return, we boarded the Spanish galley.

The archbishop, standing erect, attired as befitted his excellency, planted his enormous crucifix between us, praying aloud at the top of his voice while we did battle with the numbed and cowardly soldiers who called for mercy, offering virtually no resistance. In a matter of minutes, the ship would be ours, ours the crucifix encrusted with jewels, ours the archbishop's fine attire.

All at once we heard a terrible roar, something between a cry or a howl pierced the air, overcoming even the noise of our musicians: the galley slaves, exploiting the confusion of the rowing officer and weary of his cruel lash, gauging from the Spaniards' extreme nervousness that we'd boarded their galley, seized and passed the overseer from one to the next, still in their chains. He was the culprit reponsible for their maltreatment, and they devoured him alive before leaving him, once his horrific lament was over, as nothing more than lifeless bare bones.

The loot was so lavish and the galley so unsuitable for pursuing turtle-fishers that we decided to return with L'Olonnais as soon as possible. Prudently, however, one of our number persuaded us to wait, believing that in the winds of the previous night he'd had an intimation of an even greater, indomitable wind: none other than the Hurricane itself. Although we were not totally convinced by his words, that very word "Hurricane" engendered so much terror in us that we obeyed his warning, although at a shamefully slow pace, and headed for dry land with our plunder, given that we were already so near to the island, to search there for a cave or another hiding-place, leaving the prisoners on the galley to drown, while we took the two canoes still in our possession for the return journey to Tortuga, intending to return later for the booty. Had we known what lay ahead, with what greater alacrity should we have heeded his words!

translated by Amanda Hopkinson

STORM 7–8/1992

Josefina Estrada was born in Mexico City in 1957. Her first book of stories, Malagato, *was published in 1990.*

Extravagant Behaviour
by Josefina Estrada

From Eccentricity to Maladjustment

One Friday afternoon, in Tacubaya, in Calle de Héroes de Churubusco, outside number 43, two women—one dark and wearing a coral pink sweater, the other with glasses and long hair —were grappling with each other whilst a thin man, with curly hair and wearing a black track suit, was doing his best to separate them. That was the scene, lasting some five minutes and played out along the length of half a block, witnessed by dozens of passers-by.

When they were opposite the wine shop, the dark woman snatched off the long-haired woman's glasses, slapped some Philadelphia cream cheese on her head, rubbed it in and then gave her hair a good long tug. After a brief exchange of accusations, the women came to some agreement and hailed a taxi. They got out on the corner of Avenida de las Torres and Retorno 57, along from Copilco, without having said a single word to each other.

Some of the witnesses to the fight knew that the protagonists in the dispute are sisters and that the man who stepped in to stop them is the boyfriend of Sabina, the dark woman. They were arguing because Bonifacia, the one in glasses, was trying to force her sister to keep her first appointment with the psychoanalyst. That was why the dark one was yelling at her, "No way! Why don't you go and see the bloody psychologist if you're so keen? You're the stubborn cow who's so dead set on taking me there. Let me get on with my life in peace! I'm sick of being your puppet, your stooge."

Sabina has a five-year-old daughter. On Monday, 31 October, Bonifacia and her sisters had gone to the children's bureau to ask for legal custody of their niece because they considered that their sister was not giving her the care she needed. The sisters stated to the lawyer at the children's bureau on Insurgentes and Monterrey that Sabina was often to be found under the influence of inhalants and solvents, not to mention her use of marijuana and her occasional bouts of heavy drinking. The lawyer determined that if in six months the defendant had shown no sign of mending her ways or of a readiness to undergo treatment, she could lose custody of her daughter and one of the sisters could then adopt the child.

The following day Sabina went to the Miguel Hidalgo police station with the intention of accusing her sisters of abduction, only to discover that the law was not in fact on her side. Her sisters say that she has accepted quite meekly the decisions taken with regard to her daughter and asks only that she be allowed to visit her.

The family cannot pinpoint exactly when Sabina crossed the border that separates eccentricity from social maladjustment. At first they thought it dated from her enrolment at the Faculty of Arts, that it was there she had got into the habit of going around saying peculiar things. One day her father, a humble tradesman, remarked, "I just don't understand why everyone who studies there ends up crazy." Sabina was captivated by the idea that they thought she was mad; her family used it to forgive all her eccentricities. And on one occasion she said as much to her father: "What do you expect from someone who's mad?" "I don't know about mad," her progenitor retorted. "You're certainly a bloody idiot!"

Five years after she began behaving oddly, Sabina gave birth to a daughter. The little girl grew up in rooms where the walls were scrawled with coloured chalk, amidst piles of bottles, rubbish, flies, books and the penetrating smell of damp. Sabina lived with a poet. "And poets," argued Sabina, "shouldn't waste their time doing housework."

For the poet and Sabina adored world literature of all ages, all cultures and all genres. Sabina identified with the best-loved characters in literature from Fuensanta to Don Quixote. And so ten years went by.

Today, in those same streets of Tacubaya, many people remember her as an adolescent, wearing high heels and a veiled hat and swathed in elegant black silk. They remember her perfect oval face, her heavy eyebrows and long lashes, her fine nose. Her elegance was the object of much admiration at the fiestas in Becerra; all eyes turned to her whenever songs were sung alluding to some dark beauty. And when Sabina danced to the music of La Sonora Santanera or of Pérez Prado, it caused the kind of rapture and excitement only a movie queen from the 1940s could have provoked.

Every time Bonifacia hears Sonia Lopez sing, it inevitably evokes the memory of Sabina as a little girl, dancing, with everyone in the neighbourhood around her, the memory of the little girl who always dreamed of getting on the programme *Child Stars* and singing *The Broken Bridge* in the style of Irma Serrano. Bonifacia remembers how Sabina always promised she would give her the bag of special sweets they presented to all the contestants. That was the first of Sabina's many dreams. Bonifacia is still waiting for the sweets her sister will win when she decides to sing life's song again.

translated by Margaret Jull Costa

The Extravagant Behaviour of the Naked Woman

The woman who walks naked through the streets of Santa María provokes astonishment in the children, delight in the men and incredulity and anger in the women. She sits down at the corner of Sor Juana Inés de la Cruz and Sabino, next to the bicycle repair shop. The children come out of the two adjacent slums and cross the street to watch her as she sniffs glue from a bag, her only possession. She doesn't seem to care that she's naked, yet neither could you say that she'd made a conscious decision to display her dark, abundant flesh.

Even when she's sitting down you can tell she's a woman of vast stature. At shoulder level, her hair is a mass of tangles that contains balls of chewing gum, bits of earth, dust and fluff. The applause and whistles of the onlookers grow louder when she opens her legs and begins to scratch herself hard in the most impenetrable part of her being. At this point, the young men, who are always hanging around, can't suppress their laughter. Instinctively, as if fearing that at any moment they too might reveal their mysteries, they finger the flies of their trousers.

And when the woman lies down and turns her back on them, the onlookers begin throwing things at her. She takes a while to react, but they all know that as soon as she sits up, she'll get to her feet and chase her attackers. And the children will then be able to see that her breasts are not, in fact, stuck fast to her ample abdomen.

Some of the smaller children go and tell their mothers that "the woman who wears no knickers or anything" is on the loose again. And their mothers forbid them to go back outside.

There was a period when she was seen by several women near where Aldama crosses Mina. Then for two years she prowled up and down Avenida Guerrero. She would go to sleep surrounded by a pile of clothes donated by well-meaning people, and which served her as both pillow and mattress. When she grew tired of her bundle of clothes, she would burn it using the same solvent she inhaled.

The huge, dark woman goes into building sites to wash. The glee of the workers reaches its height when she bends over to drink from the tap. They get beside themselves with excitement when she picks up handfuls of lime and powders her armpits. Any man bold enough to approach her has always been repelled by the ferocity of her insults. The women who live around Calle Sor Juana complain not about the exhibition she makes of herself but about the fact that she's freer than the men. Instead of putting an end to the extravagant behaviour of this woman—which arouses lewd thoughts even in the most saintly of men—the police, they say, spend all their time arresting drunks.

translated by Margaret Jull Costa

THE QUEEN OF TLATELOLCO

Before the earthquake, Niños Héroes de Lerdo 307 in Tlatelolco was a thirteen-storey building, containing eighty flats. At present they are still carrying out repair work on the six storeys that remain. Now that it has been cut down to less than half its previous height, it is almost impossible to imagine La Española living there in that empty space, given her bearing and the elegance of her clothes. She was tall and had a sharp nose and heavy eyebrows, and always wore her hair up in a bun. She was what you might call a woman of a certain age. Nothing in her appearance let her down; she greeted everyone by their surname. She lived in a flat on the thirteenth floor, on the right-hand side.

One day she began wandering about the building, as if she were patrolling it, on the look-out for any "suspicious characters". She argued that the police in the lodge at the entrance didn't bother to patrol the actual building and that their presence was, therefore, pointless because they didn't keep an eye on the people inside, on the ones you really needed to watch, because some, according to her, were dangerous. Needless to say, everyone avoided her; any encounter with the woman meant having to submit to the third degree.

She also started watching the caretakers and was constantly pestering them with complaints. Everywhere she saw grime, which, in her opinion, the caretakers were determined to preserve. One day, weary of asking them to whitewash the corridor floor on the thirteenth storey, she herself painted the steps leading up to her apartment black, in a bid both to conceal the dust for good and to make it easier to detect the tracks of anyone daring to set foot in her domain.

At one time the other tenants asked the caretakers to get rid of the climbing plants in the lobby because La Española insisted on watering them day and night by hurling bucketfuls of water down on them from the thirteenth floor.

In the months prior to the earthquake, everyone in the building was puzzled by the recurring presence of excrement or urine in the lifts. At first they thought that someone from the street must have been "caught short" and what better solution than to relieve oneself in a lift. On that occasion the other tenants asked La Española to redouble her vigilance. She never found the guilty party and several tenants were convinced that it was in fact she who had taken to relieving herself in the lift. La Española could not bear to have any kind of "filth" in her own home.

This is not to say she was not kind: one day she found two homeless kittens and put them in her car; she provided them with a box to sleep in and every evening she could be seen playing with them. She fed them on tuna and ham. She hardly ever used her car at that time and did so even less once the cats, in just three months, had managed to turn it into a real pigsty.

The nineteenth of September arrived. The engineers from the Department for Town Planning and the Environment declared the building unfit for human habitation. From that night on, when utter darkness reigned, La Española slept on the thirteenth floor with her retinue of cats.

When the eviction order came, she refused to comply. The building workers arrived to demolish her flat and put all her belongings out in the street. But nothing could trouble her now. Since the earthquake, La Española had been the sole queen and mistress of Tlatelolco. To her mind she had succeeded, by sheer willpower, in ridding the place of the dangerous characters who, until then, had prevented her from living life in peace.

translated by Margaret Jull Costa

Juan Villoro was born in Mexico City in 1956. He is the author of two collections of stories (La noche navigable *1980 and* Alberras *1985), two chronicles* (Tiempo Transcorrido *1986 and* Palmeras de la brisa rápida, un viage a Yucatan *1989) and a book for children* (Las golosinas secretas). *He has translated Graham Greene, Truman Capote, Arthur Schnitzer, and Gregor von Rezzori into Spanish.*
Here, Villoro describes a group of young, urban Mexicans who head into the desert to sample the hallucinogenic plant, peyote, which is traditionally used by Mexican Indians once only to induce a mystic state of expanding concsiousness in the passage to manhood; part of the ritual is each young man going into the desert alone to find "his" peyote and going through the drug-induced stages of nausea, psychedelic visions and finally spiritual awakening which can last twelve hours or more before the rite of passage is complete.

COYOTE
by Juan Villoro

Hilda's friend, who had taken the fast train himself, waxed lyrical about leisure: they would cross the desert inch by inch, and hours later the horizon would no longer lie beyond the window but before their very faces, reddened reflections of the land where the peyote grows. Pedro thought him a moron, but this was confirmed too late, when they had already taken his advice.

They boarded the last train in a village where the tracks ploughed on to the end of the world. It was a wooden carriage full of live birds. The smell of droppings predominated until someone took a piss at the back. The seats were packed with women, their youth deadened by the dust, their eyes blank with loss of expectation. They were like a by-product of the desert that had been picked up and was now being conveyed toward some obscure extermination. A soldier nodded over his rifle. In an attempt to salvage something from all this misery, Julieta began to talk about magic realism. Pedro wondered when exactly he had begun to see such a fool as a valued friend.

In fact, the expedition had begun to lose its charm ever since Hilda had produced Alfredo. People who dress all in black are usually either withdrawn to the point of monomania, or else shameless exhibitionists. Alfredo gave the lie to both extremes. Everything about him eluded snap definitions: he wore a pony tail, he was a lawyer—international narcotics—and he took natural drugs.

There were six of them, counting him: Clara and Pedro, Julieta and Sergio, Hilda and Alfredo. They met for supper in a place where the crêpes tasted like denim. Sergio blamed the flour, being expert on such things. He announced that he wouldn't be taking any peyote himself. After ten years of psychotropic experiences, including a friend jumping off the pyramid in Tepoztlán and four months in a San Diego hospital, he'd had his fill of provisional paradises.

"I'll come up for the ride, but I'm not touching that stuff."

He was the ideal person to watch over the rest of them. Sergio was the type who finds a use for things he's never even seen, and whips up exquisite dishes from mouldy vegetables.

His wife Julieta wrote plays that in Pedro's opinion were immoderately successful. He had scorned every one of her offerings until they reached their three hundredth performance.

Alfredo left the table for a moment (to pay the bill, with his silent trick of taking decisions for everyone) and Clara leaned towards Hilda to say something in her ear, making them both squeal with laughter.

Pedro watched Clara's happiness at the prospect of going to the valley with her best friend, and felt the intense echo of witnessing something good and yet irreparable. Clara's enkindled eyes did not include him, and to taste something of her joy became a way of hurting himself. A memory pricked him with its far-off pleasure: Clara overwhelmed by their first encounter, open to the future and its promises, her life still intact.

For weeks that felt like months, Pedro had fought the idea of going back. Surely it was a contradiction to perform an initiation rite twice over. What was the good of pursuing the magic they had worn out in two years of living together? Once, in another century, they had made love to one another in the soaring desert: what had drained the energy they shared then, the naked wholeness of those hours, perhaps the only time in which they had existed outside consequence, with no ties except to each other? That afternoon, in a city of many streets, they had quarrelled over a ruined umbrella. On a clear day! What did their carping, their cramped flat, their broken appliances have to do with the bare desert paradise? No, there was no going back. And yet, faced with Clara's smile and her child's eyes bewitched by the world, he knew he would go back; seldom had he desired her so strongly, although nothing harder than being with her just then. Clara was somewhere else, outside herself, into the trip that had, in a sense, already begun.

The idea of taking the slow train was easily accepted: as pilgrims, they must choose the most arduous path. All the same, after half a day of sweltering it seemed a fatal choice. That was when Alfredo started talking about the express, Pedro cut him off by glaring. Hilda gnawed on her nails till they bled.

"Calm down, silly," said Clara.

In the next village Alfredo got off to buy juice: six cellophane bags full of whitish water, which everyone drank regardless.

The earth, sometimes yellow, most often red, slid past the windows. By afternoon they could see the jagged outline of the cliffs surrounding the entrance to the valley. They were moving so slowly that their destination, petrified in the distance, became an additional torture.

The train stopped beside an iron shack in the middle of nowhere. Two men climbed on, carrying high-calibre rifles.

After half an hour—a period that was but a moment in the dilation of the journey—the men negotiated their way round the slumped bodies in the corridor and stopped beside them.

Julieta had finished her juice: the slack bag was warming between her fingers. One of the men pointed at it, turning towards Sergio.

"How about something stronger, eh?"

The canteen went from mouth to mouth, a smarting gulp of mezcal.

"Going to shoot deer?" asked Sergio.

"Anything that moves," the man said, jerking his thumb at the land where nothing, absolutely nothing, stirred.

The sun had worked in strange ways on the hunters' faces, patchily burning the skin so that their cheeks were blotched with veins, and their necks purple. Though they had almost nothing to say, they strained to say it, falling over each other to talk small game with Sergio and, eyeing the women, anxious to know whether this was a "camping" party.

It was obvious from Hilda's dark glasses that it was going to be a peyote party.

"Those Huichol Indians don't take trains. They walk, all the way from the coast," said the hunter with a hint of aggression.

Pedro was not the only one aware of Hilda's Walkman. What could be more ludicrous than six spiritual tourists? They would no doubt get the worst of all this fraternizing, but as on so many unlikely occasions, it was Julieta who saved the day. Blowing her fringe aside, she enquired about gold-panners. One of the hunters pulled off his baseball cap and rubbed his scalp.

"People who rinse sand in rivers to find gold," explained Julieta.

"No rivers around here," the man said.

The absurd exchange continued, with Julieta plotting a scene for her next play.

The hunters were headed for a canyon known as "Get out if you can".

"Just over there," they nodded, holding their palms upright with the fingers pointing nowhere in particular.

"Look." And they proffered the telescopic rifle sights: rocks, very far away, air quivering in the notched circle.

"Are there still any boar?" Sergio asked.

"Hardly any."

"Pumas?"

"That'll be the day."

What creature might justify the effort to reach this canyon? A couple of hares, a quail perhaps?

They left as darkness was falling.

"Here. Might come in handy."

Pedro hadn't said a word. He was so startled at being the one chosen for the gift that he couldn't refuse. It was a mountain knife, with an inscription cut into the blade: I BELONG TO MY OWNER.

Twilight rewarded their ordeal. The sky was a deep blue, resolved into a single stroke of scarlet.

The train pulled up in a hollow blurred by night. Alfredo recognized the stop.

There wasn't even a zinc roof in sight. They indulged the painful relief of stretching their legs. A kerosene lamp swung from the departing engine, as if waving goodbye.

The darkness was so intense that it swallowed up the tracks within three yards. But they put off lighting the torches: insect noises, the nagging of an owl. A landscape, contemplated in all its inertia throughout the burning day, was returning to the minutiae of life. In the distance were sparks that might have been fireflies. There was no moon, only glittering trails of sand in the sky. They had done well, after all. They had arrived by the right door.

Torches were switched on. Alfredo led the way to a recess scattered with ashes.

"It's more sheltered here."

Only then did Pedro begin to sense the insidious wind that was tugging at the small round shrubs.

"They call them the witch-winds," said Sergio, starting to collect pebbles and twigs. He built a sumptuous fire which would have taken Pedro hours to make.

Clara wanted to spot constellations, knowing they would get no further than Orion's Belt. Pedro kissed her: a warm tang of mezcal lingered on her cool, moist tongue. They stretched out on the rough ground and he thought he saw a shooting star.

"Did you see that?"

Clara had dropped off on his shoulder. He stroked her throat and the soft skin made him feel the grit on his fingers.

He woke very early. The back of his neck was like stone. The remains of the fire gave off a woody scent. The sun had not yet risen in the pale blue sky.

Shortly afterwards the six of them were having coffee, the only nourishment they would take all day. The others looked happy, though strained by the discomfort of the journey, the hard cold night, and the cactus fence where they had to pee and defecate. Hilda looked as though she hadn't slept in aeons. She held up two aspirins and downed them with her coffee.

"Goddamn mezcal," she said.

Alfredo rolled up his blanket with the tip of his boot and tossed it over his shoulder, with the archetypal gesture of a cowboy in a commercial.

Pedro remembered the hunters. What were they after in this wasteland? As if reading his thoughts, Alfredo said something about caged animals shipped to foreign zoos.

"They even take the roadrunners." He brushed his hair irritably and tied it back, pointing at a towering cactus: "The Japs pull her up, roots and all, and West Pacific here we come."

His desk was piled with such cases. Who sued, the owner of the desert, the impossible sentinels of this waterless waste?

Pedro started walking. Clara's kiss evaporated in an instant, leaving a smudgy sensation in his mouth. He breathed in the clean, burning, intolerable air. They each had to find their own head of peyote, the pale-green rosette that hid itself from the unworthy. Images of the plundered desert revolved in his mind.

He was entering an area of thorny huizache and mezquite trees: ahead, a hill that would be his landmark. "The air in the desert is so pure that everything seems nearer." Who'd told him that? He trudged on without getting any closer to the hill. He set himself a more accessible goal, a tree that had been split by lightning. The cactuses made it impossible to walk straight; he sidestepped countless clusters of them before reaching the dead stump, crawling with red ants. He took off his straw hat as though the tree still gave any shade. His hair was dripping wet. At a moderate though incalculable distance the hill rose, its flanks shimmering blue. He got out his flask, rinsed his mouth and spat.

He walked on, and after a while began to feel the benefits of the sun: it cooked you, mercilessly, until there were no more thoughts or words in your head. A buzzard pinned to the sky, prickly pears like clots of blood. The hill was nothing but an expanse smeared with blue, green and brown.

Feeling hot rather than tired, he climbed fast, pouring with sweat. At the top, he stared at his sodden ankles and the socks made him think of tennis broadcasts, commentators going on about dehydration. He lay down in a clearing free of thorns. A sour, strong, sexual smell wafted from his body. He had a flashback to the hotel room in some dilapidated bit of the tropics where he had copulated with a nameless woman. The smell of damp sheets and alien, irreconcilable bodies, of the bed where she met him with violence, merging into the fire that obliterated her face.

In what corner of the desert was Clara sweating now? He had no more energy for thought, and stood up. The valley spread away, hacked with shadows. A harsh immensity of wounded vegetation. Packed and angular, the clouds hovered in stiff formation. They didn't intercept the sun, only shed oily stains over the high desert. There was a moving line of dots very far away. People, probably. Huicholes following their maracame priest. The five blue altars guarded by the divine stag were around here somewhere. Tonight they would perform the fire ritual, the incineration of words. What was the point in being here, miles from the ceremony? Two years earlier at a friend's hacienda they had drunk peyote shakes with the fervour of converts. After the purgative stage of throwing up ("This has got to be a Mexican drug," Clara had wailed) their breath smelled thick and grassy. By the time they'd decided that this was going to be nothing but vomit and pain, the prodigy overtook them for a few hours: a pristine cerebral electricity, asterisks, spirals, stars of pink and yellow and baby blue. Pedro had gone outside to take a leak and gaze at the village some way away, with its fluorescent walls. The stars had melted and the trees throbbed. He snapped a branch between his fingers and felt master of some precise power. Clara was waiting for him inside, and for the first time he knew that he stood, physically, between her and the cold, her and the limitless earth: life became a kinship of blood, the fields gave off a fresh, exultant smell, the hearth glimmered in a girl's eyes.

Was he still connected to those nights of his life, to the burning body between his hands in that forgotten port, to Clara's eyes by that fire? For that matter, had he anything to do with the city that had so painstakingly crushed them beneath its load of duties, fractured timetables and useless buttons? Clara could only conceive of one way out: going back to the valley. So here they were, surrounded by earth, their spirits a little limp from weariness and the sun that blotted out thought from time to time.

The procession forged on in the distance, followed by a curtain of dust.

Pedro turned to look the other way. At an almost unimaginable distance, he could make out some coloured flecks that must be his friends. He decided to move on. The hill would orient him, and in a few hours he'd be back to share the trip with the others. Meanwhile, though, he would steep himself in this pathless immensity, studded with cactuses and minerals, open to the wind and the clouds that could never mask it.

He scrambled down the slope and into a huizache wood. Perspective abruptly vanished into close-up: small birds hopping from nopal to nopal, purple or yellow tuna fruits. He pictured the direction the Huicholes were taking, drawing a mental straight line that cut through the vegetation, and tried to correct his round-about route. The task of getting round the magueys was so absorbing that he almost forgot about the peyote: at one point his hand brushed against the bag tied to his belt, a burning, irksome scrap of plastic.

He reached a place where the ground was

sandier: the cactuses thinned out into a clearing dominated by a great rock, a hexagonal boulder, smoothed by the wind. Pedro walked up to it: the top was at chest level. It was odd not to find ashes, crumbs, paint marks or any other sign that others had yielded to the stone's attraction before him. He hoisted himself up, scraping his arms, to examine the surface. He knew nothing about stones but sensed some ideal of abstract perfection being enacted on this spot. The rock bestowed order upon the scattered cactuses, as if to embody a different, flat, unanswerable logic. Nothing could be less comforting than those keen-edged slabs. The rock served no purpose, but its crude simplicity was a compelling symbol of the functions it might be bent to: a table, an altar, a cenotaph.

He lay back on the stone hexagon. The sun was very high now. His brain felt like flint, almost inert. Hat over face and eyes shut, he still saw a vibrating yellow film. He started worrying about sunstroke and sat up: the thorn trees had gained irridescent halos. He looked about him, the hill had disappeared.

At what point had he been enticed by the terrain into this gully? Pedro had no idea which side of the rock he had climbed. He searched for his own footprints. Nothing. Not a plume of dust to indicate the position of the pilgrims. His heart was beating thickly. He had got lost in the motionless drifting of this stone raft. Seized by a dizzy urge to jump down and plunge through any of the surrounding green walls, he hunted for some sign, some token of his route to the rock. A grey, artificial spot on the ground brought him back to his senses. A button! It had come off his shirt as he scaled the boulder. He slithered down to rescue the plastic disk, which seemed delightful to the touch. Hours in the desert, and he'd found nothing but this piece of his own clothing. At least he knew where he'd come from. He marched resolutely towards the uneven, prickly horizon that stood for return.

Once more, though he tried to stick to an imaginary straight line, he couldn't avoid making detours. The vegetation was closing ranks, perhaps there was some hidden humidity about: the organ cactuses rearing up overhead, in a chaos that parted and fused over and over. He cut slantwise, ducking under the switches of bishop's weed without ceasing to scan the small cactuses dotting the ground.

He wavered in his route: this stiff tangled collage of cactuses hadn't been there before. His one thought was to get out, into some paradise with fewer cactuses, when he skidded into something round which had a double row of thorns that made him think with ludicrous precision of the model of a flu virus he'd seen in a museum. Its spikes went into his palms. Fat spikes that were easily removed. He wiped off the blood against his thighs. What the hell was he doing here, being reminded of a vinyl virus by some nameless vegetable?

It took him a while to find a sabila plant, and by then the blood had dried. Even so, he got out the mountain knife, cut off a shoot and spread the soothing sap over the wounds.

At some point it occurred to him that he hadn't relieved himself all day. Dried out by sweat, it was hard to expel even a few drops. He paused to hack off a couple of prickly pears. One of the few things he knew about the desert was that its skin was fuzzed with invisible spines. He split the fruit with his knife and sucked greedily. Then he realized he was dying of hunger and thirst.

Occasionally the sweet afterbreath of the tunas welled up in a burn that was the only bearable thing in all this godforsaken solitude. The cactuses were seducing him into a course that might amount to a single, cunning curse. The thought of tramping around in an infinite circle made him cry out, in the knowledge that no one could hear.

When the sun was going down, he saw the leap of a hare and the scuttle of quails, quick animals that had hidden from the heat. He made out an area of scrub a few yards away, and felt an urge to collapse onto the lumpy sand. Only a lunatic would dare disturb the hours that were the desert's real night, its fiery repose.

Then he kicked a pebble, and another; the earth was drying up, becoming a rasping sound beneath his feet. He was able to walk a stretch without dodging a single bush, across a zone that was as good as a way out in this elemental world. Drained, he knelt down with a relief that in some humiliating primal way had to do with the thinning out of nopal around him.

When he got back to his feet the sun was fading into the distance. A fringe of green swam into view, surely a phantom of his charmed brain. He waited for it to dissolve. A nopal fence, a constructed, definite row, a planted field, an enclosure. He ran to see what lay on the other side and was met by desert, a desert identical to the one stretching to infinity behind him. The partition was merely a hinge for their mirror images. He sat on a stone and looked back at the other desert, with the gloom of one appreciating a senseless miracle.

He closed his eyes. The shadow of a bird flicked over him like a caress. He went on for a long time, amazed that his body could still give up so much moisture.

When he opened his eyes the sky was deepening. A watery star glimmered far away.

He heard a shot.

The fact that someone, somewhere close at hand, was killing something filled him with a sudden, bestial exultation. He let out a yell, or tried to, a toneless roar as if his throat were clogged with dust.

Another shot. Then, smug silence. As he dragged himself in the direction of the sounds, the relief of finding another person began to be tempered by the fear of providing them with a target. Perhaps he was not tracking the noise of a gun, but only its echo gone astray in the desert. Were any of his senses to be trusted? He kept crawling all the same, scraping his knees and forearms, afraid of an ambush but more afraid of arriving too late, to find nothing but a trail of blood. He found himself surrounded by low shrubs and silence.

He raised himself slightly to look around: a ring of black birds was hovering at what seemed an accessible distance. He stood up and walked on.

He passed into a region of utter aridity, like a fossilized limestone sea. Here and there thistles offered up their exhausted stems. The circle of birds melted into a sky where it was hard to make out anything but stars.

In his ludicrous plight, any change was for the better: it gave him as much pleasure to see the shadows of thornbushes as breaking free of the green maze had done before.

He headed for the curtain of shadows, where the darkness made him overlook the cactus pieces littering the ground. A nopal leaf bit into his foot like a second sole. He prised it off with the knife, eyes swimming in tears.

After a while he was surprised to find how easy it was to walk with a wounded foot: any other sensation was drowned out by weariness. He reached the spiky huizache branches but there was no time to get his breath. Beyond, in a ravine, were torches, fires, intense activity. He remembered the Huichole and their rite of fire. An intricate randomness had made him stumble on the pilgrims. Then a great shadow disturbed the desert with a piercing screech. Pedro now saw the crane, the tense pulleys brandishing a monstrous contraption, a plant bristling with extremities that the night turned into lunging tentacles. The men down there were uprooting an organ cactus. Pedro was unmoved. In all the day's chaos, to confuse Huicholes with plant robbers was only a minor setback. He had made up his mind to approach when a shot rang out. There were shouts from below, the cactus rocking in the air, men kicking dirt over fires, disjointed shadows everywhere.

Pedro flung himself flat onto some decayed, stinking compost. Another shot froze him into the putrescence. The camp was returning the fire. The word "crossfire" floated up from some recess of his brain, that was where he was, on the line where attack merged with defence. He prayed on his shadowy mound, knowing that after the shoot-out he couldn't risk meeting either of the two sides.

Later, as he was moving aimlessly on, he wondered whether he was leaving the bullets behind or walking right into another obscure gunfight.

He lay down, eyes nailed open by the tight muscles of exhaustion, and realized with infinite sorrow that closing them was the only home coming left. He didn't want to picture Clara's soft hands, or the firelight which his friends were sitting in, worrying about him; he couldn't give in to the madness that concocted such a precise fantasy out of his return.

Though he'd become used to the dark, he did not see at first, so much as sense a proximity. A warm body had invaded the shadows. He turned, in slow motion, trying to muffle his excitement, neck twisted out of joint, blood slamming in his throat.

Nothing could have prepared him for this: a coyote on three legs was watching him with bared teeth, an even drone, almost a purr, coming from its clamped jaws. The animal was bleeding—Pedro couldn't take his eyes from the raw stump of leg. He edged one hand towards the knife and the coyote was on him. The fangs were enmeshed in his fingers. He managed to shield himself with his left hand while the right fought through and unbearable thrashing of legs to a spot where he drove the knife strongly in and slit the three-legged beast. He felt the blood gush over his chest, the teeth release their grip. A soft flick of the tongue caressed his neck in parting.

Strange energy charged through him: he had survived, hand to hand. He wiped the blade clean and tore off his shirt for bandages. The beast was lying, massively, over a black stain. He tried to lift it and failed. Kneeling, he drew out fistfuls of hot entrails and felt overwhelmed with the relief of sinking his aching hands into such moistness. The battle with the coyote had lasted seconds, but he struggled for hours with the corpse; at last he managed to get the skin off, though he couldn't be sure of the results, he hoisted it over his shoulders and set off again.

Exhilaration only lasts a moment: Pedro could no longer describe the feeling, but pressed on, still ablaze with that moment, his strength renewed, breathing in the powdered-metal, acidic breeze.

He looked at the stars. Somewhere, elsewhere, Clara would also be staring at the unknown sky.

Every now and then he bumped into branches that were probably covered in thorns. He was at the limits of his endurance. Something pierced his thigh. He yanked it out without stopping. At one point he noticed that the knife was out of its sheath: a senseless glare was trembling on the blade. It was all he could do to put it back, having lost control of the most elementary actions. He collapsed onto the ground. Before or after falling asleep he saw the vault of the stars, like a glittering arena.

He woke with the coyote hide glued to his back; in the midst of a pungent smell. It was dawn. His mouth tasted salty. He heard buzzing very close by, and stood up in a cloud of flies. The desert thrummed, a blurred space. The effort to focus on the promontory in the distance dampened some of the joy he felt at finding he'd got back to the hill.

He reached the slope by midday. The sun burned straight down and his temples were beating feverishly, but even so the view from the top was crystal clear: the other valley and two plumes of smoke. The camp.

He set off towards his friends, at a pace that in him seemed lively but was no doubt a crawl. He arrived at nightfall.

After so long adrift in a land of green and brown, the sight of bright shirts was an unspeakable pleasure. He hollered, or tried to. A parched moan made Julieta turn around and then she screamed.

He was still until he heard purposeful steps approaching: Sergio, the protector, with a look of intense reproach, and Clara, her face white from the sleeplessness of waiting.

Sergio halted a few yards away, perhaps so that Clara could be the first to embrace him. Pedro closed his eyes in anticipation of her touch. When he opened them, Clara was still transfixed three uncrossable steps away.

"What have you done?" she said in a tone of weary disbelief verging on disgust.

Pedro swallowed thick saliva.

"What the hell is that?" said Clara, motioing towards the skin over his shoulders.

He remembered last night's combat and tried to convey his obscure triumph: he had prevailed, he bore the trophy! But he only managed a confused shrug.

"Where have you been?" Sergio stepped closer.

Where? Where? Where? The question ricocheted through his brain. Where had the others been? Where was this hallucination being acted out? Pedro collapsed onto his knees.

"It's revolting! Why, for Christ's sake?" Clara's voice was becoming corrosive.

"Give me the flask," Sergio ordered.

He felt a cold spurt and licked the water running down his face, tasting the sour tang of his blood mixed with that of the animal.

"Let's get that shit off him," said a deliberate voice, able to pronounce the word "shit" with infinite decorum.

He felt as if a scab were being wrenched off. The coyote skin fell around his knees.

"What a godawful stink."

A slow silence settled. Clara knelt beside him without touching him watching him from a distance. Sergio was back with a spade.

"Bury it, man" he said, tapping him on the back of the head, the first touch since the fight with the coyote, a contact of electrifying gentleness. "Leave him alone."

They went away.

It was getting dark. He fingered the skin that had been his companion in the desert, smiled and felt a stabbing pain across his cheekbones. Any unnecessary gesture had become a way of squandering life. He looked up. The sky was once more filling with unknown stars. He began to dig.

He tossed the shapeless mess into the hole and patted the earth carefully over it, making a soft mound with his wounded hands. He lay back, resting his head against it. Just before falling asleep he heard a whimper, but it was too late to open his eyes. He was back. He could sleep. Here. Now.

translated by Lorna Scott-Fox

Enrique Serna was born in the Federal District of Mexico in 1959. He is the author of two novels (El ocaso de la primera dama *1987,* Uno soñaba que era rey *1989), and a book of stories,* (Amores de segunda mano *1991).*
In this prurient tale of desire and unabashed need, an ageing cabaret star confesses to a lifetime of lascivious evenings, and makes a strange request...

An Artist's Sustenance

by Enrique Serna

You'll wonder how I can be so daring, you'll ask what has a garrulous old cigar-seller like me has been smoking, but I want you to do something rather special, how shall I put it, an odd favour. I can't bear misunderstandings and would rather begin from the beginning and put you in the picture. You look like a kind person, that's why I dared to bother you. I don't tell my life story to anybody, just to educated people, who have lived, who obviously understand matters of the heart.

As I was saying, soon after leaving Pinotepa, some twenty years ago, I worked here in the Sarape club, when cabaret was something else. We had a quality show and choreographed our own dance routines, not like today when the girls come out and strip naked as the day they were born. I don't mean to insult the girls, but in the old days we respected our public, and loved the profession. Obviously our clients were different, tourists from all over the world—Swiss, French, English—so it was a pleasure to go on stage. Don't think I don't understand the girls today. Why cast pearls to swine? The public in Acapulco still behaves, but those who come from Mexico City make me feel like kicking them out, they come just to annoy us artists, shout obscenities, and worst of all, they never go off with any of us. What the hell do they come here for?

Well, you'll never guess that this very person talking to you now once had a fantastic body. I used to begin with an Afro-Caribbean number, you know the thing, shaking my hips, rolling on the ground like a lizard, shuddering all over, like Tongolele used to, only more wild. I was a great hit, and should have been the star of the show. I knew this because men watched me in silence, dumbfounded by their lust, while whenever Berenice, the supposed star of our show, took off some of her clothes the men shouted things like, "Hey little mamma!", "Tasty cunt!", or "I'll set you up in a flat!"—which meant she made men nervous because she had no real skills and, poor thing, didn't know how to move her body. Her skin may have been creamy white and her hair platinum blonde, but as for her artistic talents—zero.

She was so jealous of me that I was forced to change my number. She couldn't stand being in my shadow. According to Don Sabás, a fat oaf who ran the cabaret but wasn't the boss (the boss was Berenice's lover, so that's how I know who was to blame) according to this pot-bellied idiot, men didn't like my number. Do me a favour! I don't have to tell you how I felt! Livid! That's what you get when you're a pro, I thought, for having an artist's soul, not a whore's. I was tempted to tell Sabás where he could get off, and everybody else for that matter, but I lit a cigar and said to myself, don't make a big fuss or you won't get a job anywhere else in the business, first listen to what fatty offers you, and if it's not insulting, accept it.

He offered me a job as partner to a dancer and we had to pretend to make love on stage. You can see this kind of show anywhere nowadays, but then it was new, he'd just seen one at Tijuana and thought it would be a smash hit. The idea didn't much appeal to me at first, I'll admit, it was like sinking from dance to porn, but I kept a grip on myself because I wanted to teach Berenice a lesson, right, screw her right on her home ground, show her that I wasn't just some acrobat. During our rehearsals my partner was a handsome dancer, Eleazar by name, I think. He was picked because he was the least effeminate of the men at El Sarape. He had docker's shoulders, a moustache and eyebrows like Pedro Armendariz. I felt sorry for that hulk of a man. The poor love couldn't react to me and we never really got started. He was freezing cold and he used to grip me with pincers not fingers, as if I'd put the fear of God in him. I need to believe in my role so that the public can sense my pleasure. Well, thank God, on our first night at El Sarape Eleazar didn't turn up. The day before he'd run off with a Yank who set him up in a penthouse in Los Angeles. The shit had a steady relationship on offer, no wonder he didn't concentrate on his act with me. We discovered all this when it was too late to cancel the show, so I was sent off to the wars, so to speak, with a replacement called Gamaliel who knew more or less what to do because he'd watched us rehearse, but he was the most effeminate of them all, really a woman. Sabás teased him by chucking some keys on the floor, as Gamaliel was always dropping them so when he bent down he could smooth his hands over his buttocks, like a proper little lady. Luckily I had a brainwave, and thought, rather than do what I had rehearsed it would be better to improvise. Don't submit to the tough guy because there are no men about, act as if you are the man, seduce the whore.

It worked wonderfully. Gamaliel was shy at first, I rubbed my tits in his face and he looked like he thought the world was going to end, and he didn't know were to put his hands. But as soon as I started screwing him slowly, almost maternally, his confidence grew. I began playing with him as if I was a tender friend and noticed that he relaxed, even enjoyed the way I ran my hands all over his body, so much so that half way through the show he took the initiative and started to pretend to penetrate me with great style, his pelvis moving in rhythm to the mambo saxophone music while I excited him with my gentle cat-like movements. Well, there was Gamaliel, lying between my legs and I was scratching him with my toe-nails when suddenly I felt something rock hard trying to push its way into me, violently. I saw that Gamaliel had another look on his face, as if he didn't know who he was, and my woman's vanity took over. I pride myself on being a bit of an expert fag-shagger and I felt really turned on, like a right lesbian—I bit Gamaliel's ear and drew blood. Thank God the music stopped, otherwise I think we would have gone the whole way in front of everybody .

The applause lasted five minutes. I remember that moment well because as we went out for the third time Gamaliel grabbed my arm and dragged me to my dressing room—he couldn't wait any longer. Neither could I, to be truthful. We fell on to the sofa, on top of all my dresses and finished off what we'd started on the stage, but this time going all the way, ripping off our tights, and still listening to the applause which echoed inside us as if the public's excitement had entered our bodies, as if the rhythmic clapping was pumping through our veins.

Gamaliel couldn't speak to me for days afterwards, he was deeply embarrassed by having lost face. Even the waiters realized what he'd done and began to tease him, saying things like, "Before you always liked it up the back passage, now it's ac/dc," and he felt so insulted that I said to Sabás, "Listen, control your people, I don't want to lose my partner because of their filthy tongues." On stage we went on coupling marvellously, but he refused to let himself go, he had an absent look in his eyes, his skin was sort of numb and he kept his distance so as not to cross the line again. I'll admit his resistance hurt my pride. Gamaliel had given me a great deal of pleasure in my dressing room and I wanted to take him there again as a trophy—but no such luck. He remained strictly a pro, deeply into his own kind, so that for a while I said to myself, forget him, he was a man for only one day.

Imagine my surprise when two months later I found him waiting outside the El Sarape doors early in the morning, completely drunk, holding a plastic rose and saying he'd waited up all night because he couldn't stand the torture of loving me any longer. They say true artists should never fall in love, but I never managed to cheat on love, which probably explains why I ended so fucked up. Gamaliel came to live with me in my room in the Oviedo Hotel. Although we saw each other every day we liked it more and more. Making love after the show became a habit, sometimes we were in such a hurry we forgot to shut the dressing-room door. And watch out if we heard applause somewhere else! God knows what got into us but when a compere on TV asked the audience to clap for Sonia Lopez or for the Rufinos we just felt our bodies on fire. Love was fine with us, but our professionalism lead us into a trap. Gamaliel turned very jealous. He didn't like me going off with clients, he wanted me to himself all the time. To top it, he got offended when the clients taunted him. The fact is he was just as effeminate in his gestures as before, and some drunks shouted obscenities like "This sauce has no chilli in it!" or, "I'll take you both home!", bloody queers, I bet they couldn't even get it up, and not one of them could have satisfied me like Gamaliel did. The day came when he lost his temper, and punched a bearded red-head who was pestering him. This red-head was a buddy of the state governor and threatened to get El Sarape closed. Sabás wanted to sack Gamaliel but I said no bloody way, fair's fair, either both of us stay, or both of us go.

We both went. Nobody around Acapulco would give us work because of what happened. We went to Mexico City and soon found a job in the Artists' Club, which was then a top-class joint. Thanks to suggestions from the manager we brought our show up to date. We now called ourselves Adam and Eve and went on stage wearing fig leaves. The musical accompaniment was excellent. It opened with harp chords suggesting pure, innocent love. When Gamaliel bit the apple I handed him, the devil got into us through frantic guitar music by Santana. We earned good money because on top of our salary they paid us to perform in orgies held for politicians. They thought they were really perverse, but they made me laugh. I felt sorry for those slobs who got all excited while we sweated away on stage. I tossed them the crumbs of my pleasure, you might say. However, Gamaliel didn't like it, and he didn't like the perverts who watched. He felt guilty, he acted like a spoilt child over anything. "We have no privacy," he'd say, "I'm sick of those shits staring at us. I bet they wouldn't like me watching them with their wives."

As we'd saved quite a bit, we decided to quit the stage. Gamaliel got a job as a manicurist with a hairdresser, I looked after our flat in Doctores and we began the normal life of decent couples, eating at home, going to the cinema, going to bed early, Sundays at La Marquesa, in fact, a wretched, miserable life. Wretched and miserable because in the end our bodies decide our fate and now Gamaliel became impotent. He made love to me once in a thousand years, and then grudgingly, as if he had to, and guess why? Because he missed the audience, he missed the applause that is the sustenance of artists. Thanks to that famous feminine intuition, I immediately realized what was happening. Gamaliel didn't want to face up to it, said not over his dead body would he return to the stage, that he enjoyed being a manicurist, so I went on suffering quietly like a good little submissive wife until I discovered that Gamaliel had reverted to his old ways, and was giving the customers at the hairdresser's the come-on.

That was the last straw. I said either we go back to the stage or we each one go our own way. I'd never seen him in such a rage. He foamed at the mouth and bit his fist, screaming how dare I try and boss him about as he wasn't interested in old hags. "Well, why did you hand me the plastic rose? Why did you come and live with me, you mother-fucker?" That soon shut him up.

Bit by bit he cooled down, then went on his knees begging forgiveness, just like in the movies, swearing he'd never leave me, even if we ended up in the filthiest brothel in hell.

As we were now well known in the capital, we did the rounds of the oil towns like Coatzacoalcos, Reynosa, and Poza Rica, where people like splashing their money about. The first years we earned stacks of cash. The problem was that Gamaliel took to serious drinking. You could tell he was drunk on stage, at times he couldn't lift me up, or he crashed into the tables. The audiences jeered. It was hard work persuading the manager not to replace him with another dancer. One night in Tuxpan this led to the scandal of the century. I'd had one too many as well and never worked out what really happened. Clearly we forgot we were in front of an audience, we thought we were back in our dressing room, and we were at it without a care in the world when some heavies climbed on to the stage and tried to rape me, sticking their things out and shouting, "I want some too, darling, give me a break." Close behind them came the cops, swinging their coshes. Christ, I was hit here, look at the scar by my eyebrow, and all hell broke loose. Someone stuck an ice-pick into one of them. So Adam and Eve ended up in jail, quite a chicken coop. "Separate them," the sergeant said, "Don't put those two together, they're like bitches on heat."

Things started to go downhill from then on. Night-club owners are a mafia, they all know each other and when there's a scandal everybody soon gets to know about it. Nobody would give us work except in fleapits in forgotten towns where you work without permits. Apart from the danger, it was humiliating to act there, especially since we'd known the best. On earth floors our show seemed so ordinary, and I got covered in cuts and sores. We tried to retire but couldn't—art is in your bones and we were stuck with the vice of needing applause. When we asked for work it was obvious that we loved the footlights too much and overnight we became beggars, eager to accept starvation wages, two or three thousand pesos a night. Nothing is worse for an artists than to have their dignity taken away from them. Remember, our way of life had disfigured our bodies. We were in our forties by now, Gamaliel had a pot belly, and I could do nothing about my cellulite. We were a complete flop. Someone said try singing instead of fucking on stage. They were right, but how could I tell them that without the applause nothing happened?

To cut a long story short, we ended up working for free. Nobody could stop us being exhibitionists. In some of the seediest joints they pitied us and let us skip the show when only a few people turned up. We earned cash selling clothes, costume jewellery and watches that we would lug from village to village. We carried on like this until one day we said, enough is enough, why travel so much when we have friends in Acapulco? Let's go and live there, and so here we have been for the last three years.

Our health, thank God, is good, and we work for Berenice who now owns El Sarape. See that old bag? That's her, sitting at the till counting her millions. Gamaliel is the man who collects the stars' high heel shoes. You've already noticed him? That silver-haired man by the curtains. Good-looking isn't he? He's forty-four, but he looks forty, or do I see him through rose-tinted glasses? Isn't it thrilling to love someone like I love him? You don't have to say anything, I could see a mile off that you're the understanding type, that's why I've trusted you with my life story.

Now I wonder if you'd do me a little favour? Just off the passage, there behind the beer crates, Gamaliel and I have a room. Here, take this, it's all I've got on me, please, it's not much, but I'm not going to ask you to do anything, really. Just come along and watch us, and, if you don't mind, clap when it's over.

translated by Jason Wilson

STORM 5:

Featuring Ben Chant
—as heard on Radio 4's
"Short Story"

THE TABLECLOTH TRICK
by Ben Chant
JUNGLE
by Svatava Antosova
WINTERLUDE
by Dean Albarelli
ST PETERSBURG
by Desmond Hogan
MARSHLAND GRASS
by Sarah Kirsch
THE ANGELS
by Sophie Basch

Carlos Chimal was born in 1954, lives in Mexico City and is a writer and editor whose books of short stories include Una bomba para Doménica *1978,* Escaramuza *1987,* Cuatros Bocetos *1983 and* Cinco del Aguila *1990, from which the following is chosen.*

SANTA
by Carlos Chimal

Ah, what a night that was! How could I ever forget it! But then at fourteen, impressions —those left deep inside you—last forever. A fortnight before, my mother had sat at her sewing machine and produced an organdie dress with an imperial waistline—terrible! My legs were very skinny, so I didn't dare take a step except to chase the kids who suddenly darted past like flashes in and out of the guests, and I felt I belonged more to the dark, lonely garden than to the glittering, lively drawing room. It had always been like that, since I'd turned twelve: my mother would always get her hopes up whenever one of her dressmaking clients invited her to a little party, and of course I was the best person to accompany her now that I was "of age". But that night was too much. To go to the wedding of one of the daughters of the owner of such-and-such shops in the city? My mother was showing off my dress, which all the ladies were fussing about and all the young girls were staring at green with envy. I wanted to vanish on the spot! And then, suddenly, the orchestra began to play *Patricia*! I was all hot under the collar at the thought of one of the boys coming up to me, taking me by the hand, and saying... But nothing happened, tan, taran, taran, taran; tan, taran, taran, taran... Without realizing it, I had begun to wiggle my large feet which were swallowed up by a pair of white yarn socks and black patent leather pumps. Then two of the boys who lived in the house (I only knew that later) came up to me, both very cute, in their little gunpowder blue suits, with their hands in their pockets and their quiffs held up by brilliantine. I was all of a flutter! One of them, the older one, said to me, "Drivel yesterday?" or something of the sort which I didn't quite catch. "What?" I asked, moving my head a bit closer without uncrossing my arms which were dripping with sweat, making me even more embarrassed; then he added, "With your mouth," and burst out laughing. Still dopey, I let out, "Huh?" And he said to me in the silly tone that they all use in Chapalita, "Huuuh? Purrr!" ending with the tip of his tongue to one side, blowing a raspberry and spraying me with his disgusting lips.

Thank God it wasn't long before the Beatles came on the scene so that, despite the niggles and scoldings, we were able to leave behind satin and tulle for denim and freedom. In fact, I'm not sure it was them, though I believe it was, because to dance to *Twist and Shout* there was no better outfit than trousers, and to shake to *Roll Over Beethoven* you had to let your hair down. Oh, it was marvellous to feel your legs swathed in floral cotton and to kick them up to the moon!

But life isn't always a bowl of cherries. I don't know how it happened, but four or five visits by my mother to that house in Chapalita were enough to get me mixed up with those two devils. They used to follow me about in the garden which surrounded the house, corner me on the verandah, and we would finish up to our necks in the swimming pool. Although, as I've said, I was terribly skinny, I had breasts already, and when I emerged from that beautiful pool my bosom, moulded in the shiny nylon, was just the sight Javier and Fernando wanted to see. They were very thin too, like beanpoles, but they had their charms. They both had full, pert bottoms, and white backs that would become broad and firm over the years, and whiter and more freckly. I remember that first night well, as I also remember another, three years later, stained on my memory like beetroot juice.

I had just turned seventeen. I was still on the slim side, but my breasts were large and round. Javier was nineteen, and Fernando eighteen. Things had not changed that much, but the clothes had, a lot. My hair reached down to my rump, and, in spite of my mother's theatrics, I would squeeze myself into jeans, wear a cotton T-shirt with no bra, and a wide brown leather belt. Javier and Fernando had hair that came down over their ears, but I never saw them in anything other than cotton drill trousers.

The Atlas Circuit festivities had been announced: its route started in Guadalajara, reached Zapopan and ended back in the outskirts of the city. That afternoon, to celebrate my birthday, we went out to the El Abajeño restaurant. I had a job by then, making up bikinis and sequin-studded clothes for starlets, so they didn't have to invite me, nor for that matter at any other time, which is I believe what saved me from all those hoodlums. The thing is that there we came across their friends, the Ruizes.

We climbed into their Cadillac and carried on drinking local tequila from a small barrel installed in the car: great fun, both the car and the tequila. Further down the road, it was all agreed: Javier and Fernando would tune up their cars and race, with all expenses paid by their friends the Ruizes. Javier had a white T-Bird, and he dived into his machine, got stuck into the suspension, and ended up with a powerful and superstable car. A speedboat, in fact. Fernando's father had given him a Corvette on condition that he wouldn't fail his first year at college, and he made the most fabulous use of the thing. He even had some bursts of flames painted on the sides, that's how he used to take his machine around.

We stayed together those weeks. We didn't leave the garage other than to cross the ironing room and go to eat in the kitchen, or to doze for a few hours in the rooms at the end of the garden, outside the house. Actually, now that I think of it, we did go out one Saturday afternoon. We couldn't miss the first live performance of our friend Manolo Muñoz, he wouldn't have forgiven us. We cheered like mad, ate meat tacos, and drank tepache in the evening in his honour.

In the house in Chapalita we didn't take any risks: his parents had gone away on a long trip and his aunt Chala, who had come from the capital to take care of them and their ten brothers and sisters, had fixed me with her eyes and asked me a few things, enough to make out my class and education. I'd never known such a lady. She was attentive, refined and self-controlled. I would have liked to have been her daughter, then they would have been my cousins and none of what followed would have, and my heart would not have been broken... The one good thing I have from those years is Alfredo, my Freddy.

The day finally arrived. Guadalajara was one big party. The presence of several international drivers, among them Moises Solana and Pedro Rodriguez, gave extra dash to the competition. Can you imagine it, a real race! Javier was dreaming of going over to the other side, not to run race tracks, but the stock exchange. On the other hand, when it came to Fernando, I even had to cool him down once, well, twice, as he was stubbornly planting himself in the middle of Indianapolis and spraying everyone with champagne. I don't know which one of them I liked better (I know that I fascinated both of them, I think they'd never had a friend like me), and my heart was pounding because I felt that I'd have to decide that night. They had sworn in the Ruizes' Cadillac that they would race for me and in these matters, there can be only one winner... Engines roared, visors dropped, arms were seen stretched tensely over steering wheels. A young girl in a tennis skirt waved the starting flag and the racing cars were away that red afternoon.

Nearly two hours later, a vehicle appeared in the distance, then another, and immediately several more. I thought my heart was going to burst, when I saw Fernando's Corvette in the lead. A man waved the black and white chequered flag with great skill and speed, leaping in the air at the finish. Fernando had won, he had beaten the great racing drivers!

I jumped for joy, but later I thought with sadness that that would be the end. Who can tell, perhaps I would get on with him (I never thought of getting married, can you believe it?). But, no. The most sensible thing would be for him to pack up his things with a juicy contract and let the track go. But, well! At that moment, in the middle of the din and confusion, I forgot everything and I ran into his arms. He kissed me on the lips. I kissed him back, and took his helmet off and sunk my fingers into his blond head of hair. Ummm... what didn't I feel here, there, and further down.

Later he told me that he was upset because just as his brother's Thunderbird had found its way to the front and was overtaking the Moises' Solana, the gearbox had broken. After the prize-giving we managed to get rid of the Ruizes, ran off to Chapalita in another car, told aunt Chala the news and went to look for Javier.

We bought some bread, a bit of ham and yellow cheese, a few cokes, and we sped off on our way. With the excuse that Javier had been left behind we took their father's Mercury—automatic from A to Z, with air conditioning and everything else thrown in. Fernando switched on the radio and we glided down the road. The night sky was clear, blue and full of stars.

Suddenly we saw, heading in the opposite direction, a tow-truck pulling another which in turn was hauling Javier's T-Bird. Fernando tooted his horn like someone possessed, but the procession continued on its way. Not knowing what to do, we stopped on the side of the road. The night was so warm and beautiful that we climbed out to watch it.

There he surprised me for the second time. He knew the names of some constellations and pointed them out. I had already noticed his powers of observation, especially when he looked at me, but I didn't know that he took notice of anything beyond his machines. He told me a story about the Milky Way and said that my eyes had fallen from the sky millions of years ago and that my mouth was unforgettable. He embraced me again and this time we didn't let go. It wasn't him who suggested the car—it was I. None of the small hotels in Zapopan could have competed with those wide leather seats and the radio music which echoed our feelings.

Afterwards, he took a box of Lucky Strike from the glove compartment and we shared a cigarette. A sheep truck hurtled past and brought us back to earth. I'm sure no one found out, but even before my belly began to swell, Javier sensed it. And Fernando too. One day we didn't see each other, nor the next, and nor on those that followed. I wasn't going to ask them for anything: with what I was earning making those minute clothes for the strippers I managed quite well, especially later when they started ordering costumes for their films. They all knew what was happening to me and they behaved impeccably. When I first became aware of it I was living in a flat in the suburb of Narvarte and, the next thing, Freddy was born.

It's for his sake that I have endured all these years, and because he has made it, that's enough about me. Now that the whole world recognizes my son, I'd like to tell you how he got where he is today.

Like any mother, I wanted to give him an education, a name, the best of everything. I wanted him to be an engineer or something, but with the constant coming and going in the film world, parties, and men… Life is easy and complicated at the same time. What it gives you, it makes you pay for. Though I can assure you that I didn't neglect Freddy, he didn't turn out very studious, as you'll see. He grew up to be a strapping young man, with a fair complexion like his father's and his eyes blue like his grandfather's (I never knew my father—my mother never mentioned him—but I'm sure that if Freddy carries something of mine, it's not my dark colouring or my black eyes, but my pride). One day, he sat beside me, rested his arm on my sewing machine and told me that he was going across the border.

I almost stuck a needle into my finger, but I took a deep breath and sent him on his way.

After a week, I received a phone call. "Ma, I'm all right here in Los Angeles, don't worry, I've already got a job," and after four days, a postcard, Sunset Boulevard on one side, and on the other, *For the most beautiful mother in the world. From her Alfredo*. After three months, a money order came for one hundred dollars. I was missing him, all the more because it was some time since I'd had a man around, not that I wanted one any more. Soon afterwards he sent me a dozen photos: Freddy with friends, on the beach, with an enormous car flush to the ground, and later the same car with the bonnet up, like a rearing horse, there was also one with a lovely young girl, and I couldn't hold back my tears. She had olive brown skin, her hair was black and thick like mine, her legs strong and shapely, the way I'd have liked mine to be. In the background you could see the entrance to Universal Studios, and in his letter he asked, *When are you coming, Ma?* When? I didn't know, it had never crossed my mind. Of course, some of the starlets I was working for were past their prime, but there were others now, some of them as young as Freddy's girl, who needed miniskirts in the morning, hot pants by the afternoon, and knitted bikinis by the evening. Who would dress them if I wasn't around?

At the end of one year, I received a letter.

Boss, it's happened. A short while ago they threw the Red Indians out from Alcatraz Island, and they say that it's our turn next. Now it's not the grown-ups who pass joints around, but children in rags. The damned blacks hate us. In the town, I sometimes get by like a ghost because of the colour of my skin, but they don't let Maria through. This is no way to go on, Ma. I felt sorry for him, and I wrote right away that he should come back home, what was he doing over there, suffering for nothing. But his reply was, *You've got me wrong, the problem is in the Deep South. I'm going up north where things will be different. I have split up with Maria because she wouldn't have a chance. She cried and made a big fuss, but I'm not going to be beaten by the gringos here —up there for sure there's equality.*

I didn't hear from him for six months. Those were grey days for me and my clients. They were shooting very few films and almost the only outlet was television. With time and by the grace of God the girls were able to recover their jobs. I thought everything was finished.

I was in that state when I received his letter

and a photo showing him in front of a house all covered in snow, with two other characters, the three of them dressed in a very peculiar manner and waving their hats at the camera. "What's this?" I asked myself, "He's dressed up like Santa Claus!" I tore open the envelope.

Did you think I'd disappeared, Ma? Here I am, alive and well and studying. I think I have finally found what I've always really wanted, and I hope you'll be pleased too, because you always wanted me to go to school. Here in Albion, N.Y. there is one that specializes in Santas. The graduates that leave here are the best in the world. As you see, I've had to fatten up a bit and grow a moustache—it's bleached but it's my own, like the beard. You've no idea how much I've learned with these good people. Apart from finding the best laugh for each occasion, we learn walking, all kinds of magic tricks and public speaking. That's very important, Ma, the whole world wants to hear Santa Claus: children, young people and adults all wait for Santa's advice. I shall receive my diploma in three months and with that I'll be able to work in the best places in New York, Chicago and Washington, not only on the streets, but also at banquets and private parties. Take care, Boss, and be happy. Best wishes, Santa.

I can't tell a lie. At first I felt unsure, just like I did that time at the Atlas Circuit before the race. I wasn't convinced that this was the best thing for Freddy, for the more I tried to imagine it, the more I couldn't help thinking of the poor bums in the Alameda park. But I cheered up when I realized that things must be different over there, and that one day Freddy would become a great Santa Claus.

That's just what happened. A few days ago I received some photos, a magazine and a video tape. I watched that first. It was marvellous to be able to see Freddy, and not just read his writing! Seated under the sunshade of a garden table, with a swimming pool in the background, he was telling me, "Ma, things could not have turned out better. After a spell in the Big Apple, I left New York for a terrific contract in Miami. Just like that. A dealer from over there liked my style, and his only request was that I should put on a bit more weight. 'No problem,' I said to him, I took the Silver Meteor and in no time established myself in the best houses. Have you seen my photo with Charles Bronson? Now I'm staying in the deluxe Palm Beach Hotel. Ma, look at those photos in the magazine, they're of the night of my success. I send you kisses. Tomorrow I'll deposit one thousand dollars in your account." The video showed him with the other hotel guests; he was always surrounded by people, being admired.

It was very moving. I leafed through the magazine: Madonna was on the front page and one of the titles read, "Christmas from Coast to Coast." I came to the part where there were several small photos of people at a party and, on turning the page, oh God! Freddy in a double-page spread, ruddy, his hair white, with glasses, hugging a man of about fifty with an enormous protuberant red nose. Like my son, after all these years I have learned a little English and I was able to read a few words of the report...

Freddy Chaste, considered in this day and age the Santa of the Stars, has just shown himself to be a fantastic host in the house of the splendid Imelda Marcos. "It's not easy," says Santa Chaste, "to be a real Santa here in Hollywood." As a new member of the Santa Stellar Circuit, which takes care of these tender and indispensable characters across the whole of the American Union, Santa Chaste says he feels very satisfied to travel first class now. "The Continentals are wonderful, but now I'm delighted with the deco cabins of Amtrak." All Santas know a trick or two, but this Santa has impressed us with his skilful hands and his friendly face. "Once in Virginia, I had the pleasure of attending a conference of Brady White's, the great Santa of the Stars, and there I heard him say that if you want to make it in Hollywood, the rule is to take risks to attain something beautiful. He showed us the pontifical party entrance. When the Pope visited L.A. they met at the airport. 'Santa Claus!' exclaimed the Pope, delighted. 'Marvellous work with the children,' he whispered, while Brady knelt in front of him."

Since then, Santa Chaste has learned to rest two fingers, like a feather, on the little ones' heads and he has perfected his pontifical entrance. He isn't worried that the constant requests may some day start bothering him. "Yesterday it was dolls and video games, today it is Mercedes Benz, divorce agreements, inheritance and diamonds." Has Santa Chaste ever been asked something impossible? Before we left, the stunning Madonna approached him, sat on his knees, and asked candidly, "Can I be a virgin this Christmas?" to which Santa replied with a smile and a touch of sadness, "Santa cannot perform miracles."

I put the magazine on one side and I felt my heart welling up with emotion. It was not dark yet and I realized that it had been several days since I'd set foot outside the door. I took a bath, fixed myself up the best I could and went out. I ordered a double tequila at the first bar I saw and thanked the Lord that my Freddy is doing well.

translated by Miriam Frank

The Credits

STORM 7–8 is published
with support from
the Arts Council of
Great Britain.

Special thanks are due to:
Antonia Byatt
John Capel
Claudia & Angel
Peter Dyer
Maria Guerra
Mary Hill
Caspar Luard
Ráoul Ortíz y Ortíz
Alejandra de la Paz
Marcela Ramirez
Esther Ronay
Patricia Scanlan
Lorna Scott-Fox
Stephen Watts
Graham Whybrow